SUDDENLY ALIVE

SKOT HARRIS

ALSO BY SKOT HARRIS

Ann Arbor South '96

Heart on the Run

<u>*The Neon Darkness Trilogy*</u>:

Snapshots at the Fontaine Motel

Neon Darkness

Suddenly Alive

SUDDENLY ALIVE
© 2019 Skot Harris

Cover design/photography: Bazil Yatez
Cover model: @aleksandramamine

First edition; written May-August 2019; London, England

ISBN 10: 169444368X
ISBN 13: 9781694443687

Also available as an eBook

FOR KARL DAVID,
who has brought me back
to life more than once.

"If I could ask a smoking gun
how it feels to hurt someone,
I would just ask you."
JESSIE WARE

KELLY

If it doesn't end in tears, it didn't matter.

Kelly's grandmother had been dead many years, but her shiny pearls of wisdom always came to Kelly whenever she needed them.

And she needed them now, because in this moment, Kelly hurt.

She was lost and didn't know what to do.

She'd cried a lot in her life—when her father attacked her mother for the last time and disappeared in 1987; when her Grandmother Rose jumped off the Ambassador Bridge after many painful years of untreated schizophrenia in 1991; when Dylan McKay's wife died on *Beverly Hills, 90210* in 1995; and when two of Kelly's so-called friends went on a murderous rampage in 1996.

All of that had ended in tears because it had mattered, like Rose said, but that didn't keep it from hurting like hell.

And Kelly was certain she was about to cry again, that this latest news would make the long list of her life's devastations.

"Kelly? Did you hear what I said?"

Kelly stared at Felix Macallum—the broad, beautiful Special Agent with the shaved head and thick stubble and brooding gray eyes she'd dated for two years. He'd helped her trust again and laugh again, and his subtle-but-electric smile made her belly flutter when she'd proudly declared for years she didn't *do* fluttering.

"Tell me it's not true," she said, desperately clinging to the possibility Felix could be wrong, even though he'd never been wrong about anything work-related before. She'd teased him for obsessively checking and rechecking facts and figures before accepting any truth.

If there was ever a time for him to be wrong or confused, Kelly wanted it to be now.

"Please, Felix. Tell me it's not true."

He took a very small step toward her, but didn't hug her or kiss her or even touch her, as if knowing she didn't need that yet.

And he was right.

She didn't want delicate handling; she never had. After everything she'd seen, she wanted nothing but straightforward truth.

So Felix cleared his throat and said, "It's true, Kelly."

"Then tell me again."

"Overstreet is dead."

A scorching heat filled Kelly's stomach and raced north, burning her throat and the tops of her ears and the back of her neck. She'd felt it when her father left and when her grandmother jumped and when her best friend Ford was killed by Fawn's shotgun.

And she felt it now.

Overstreet is dead.

Frank Overstreet was dead.

The handsome late-fifties FBI agent had saved Kelly's friends, Jill and Matt, from Berger and Fawn's crime spree almost a decade ago, when they were all freshly eighteen and in over their heads.

He'd since become one of Kelly's dearest friends.

He'd helped her sign an insanely lucrative publishing deal for her book, telling her friends' violent and heartbreaking story; he'd travelled on the promotional tour with her; he'd toasted her success with champagne after the millionth sale.

They'd spent their eighth consecutive Thanksgiving together a week ago, and she'd already bought him a season pass to his favorite golf course for Christmas, like every Christmas. It sat in a gold-leaf envelope on her desk, signed: *From your favorite loudmouth.*

He'd made her laugh.

He'd been her friend.

And now he was dead.

Frank Overstreet was *dead.*

"Kelly?" Felix's deep voice disrupted her daze.

Kelly stared at him.

Overstreet had introduced them. *'He'll be able to handle a spitfire,'* he'd told her, and he'd been right. Felix could handle Kelly's everything and, together with Overstreet, she'd never felt so loved and understood and supported by two incredible men in her life.

Overstreet is dead.

Kelly's vision blurred with tears. The burning, scorching heat was ready to engulf her, but she wouldn't let it, not until she had answers.

"What happened?" she asked, her throat scratchy and dry.

Felix stared at her, obviously withholding specifics.

"*What*, Felix? Tell me! Please!"

"He was killed. His body was found in Detroit early this morning."

Kelly leaped off the couch, ran to the kitchen and puked in the trashcan, releasing painful, heavy heaves onto an old copy of the Malibu neighborhood watch newsletter. She'd been annoyed at their instructions to follow a neighborhood-wide color pallet for curbside flowers. Those instructions seemed so silly and pointless now.

Felix followed her and closed the space between them to hold her long dark hair away from her beautiful face as she vomited, but he didn't patronize with soft *shhs* or *there-theres*. He just let her puke.

After she'd heaved that morning's peanut butter bagel and strawberry-banana smoothie, Kelly rinsed her mouth with water and leaned against the kitchen counter.

Still, Felix didn't speak. He folded his arms across his broad chest and leaned on the opposite counter near the window that overlooked the lush orange and lemon trees lining the bricked driveway.

Kelly stared at him, her face wet with tears.

Because it mattered.

Overstreet *mattered*.

"He was murdered?" Kelly asked in a cracked whisper.

Felix nodded.

Kelly paced the floor and pulled back her hair back with a black elastic band from her wrist. She wandered into the foyer, a great vantage point near the front door where she could see through the front and rear windows of the house.

Beyond the living room and back deck, she watched waves hit the sandy beach. She'd spent most of her book sales on this house—her Barbie Dream House—five years ago. Overstreet had helped her move vintage sixties furniture and expensive flat-screen televisions into it and he'd slept in the spare bedroom countless times.

Now he'd never set foot inside it again.

"Do you know who did it?" Kelly wiped her face, although tears came faster then she could wipe.

"No." Felix was kind and matter-of-fact as usual.

That kindness reminded Kelly of Overstreet and had attracted her to Felix. The men were similar in a lot of ways—skilled, smart, handsome, driven, bone-dry senses of humor, *kind*.

And outside of investigating and apprehending criminals, they had no known enemies. Felix was relatively new to the FBI, having ranked six years earlier at age twenty-four, and he'd sought out Overstreet. He'd wanted to be trained by the best in Detroit, and Overstreet was the best, having served nearly thirty years in the bureau. Overstreet had trained Felix and he'd liked Felix's character, hence why he'd introduced him to Kelly. Overstreet had even helped Felix transfer to the Los Angeles Field Office two years prior, so the *blossoming lovebirds* could be together.

Neither man was unfair or brutal in their positions. They treated everyone—including criminals—fairly, whenever possible.

Kelly herself had worked with Overstreet on several cases over the years, whenever he'd needed a young adult's perspective or advice. After the fierce determination she'd shown during the investigation into her friends' crime spree in '96, Overstreet had told Kelly her intuition was strong, that she would've been a good law enforcer, and that she had an investigative knack.

But in all the cases they'd studied together since as a unique redo of *Starsky and Hutch*, as Kelly had coined them—him leading the investigation, her giving female insight or using her ridiculously extensive pop culture knowledge to decipher clues—Kelly never saw criminals lash out or threaten revenge against Overstreet, at least not outside a few *Fuck yous!* or an occasional thrown fist. Overstreet was calm and kind, but authoritative and serious. She'd actually seen gangbangers and rapists and killers tremble at the sight of him.

But obviously she was wrong. At least one person had had a vendetta against him, a *reason* to want him dead.

But who?

Who the fuck did this?

Overstreet had been *softly retiring*, as he'd called it, slowly making his exit by finishing paperwork and the boring busywork he'd avoided for too long. He hadn't worked on an active investigation for six months, his last case involving a young man who'd jumped to his death from a Marina del Rey apartment balcony to escape a killer. But Overstreet had handed off that case before returning to Michigan, so there were no active cases or immediate signs of motive.

"Was it random?" Kelly asked Felix. "A mugging? A robbery?"

"No," he answered. "It was not random."

"How do you know?"

"Because of the . . . *condition* of his body. We've seen it before."

Every inch of Kelly hurt—her eyes from crying, her throat from puking, her veins from racing adrenaline. She'd spent nearly a decade using her book as an educational tool, schooling young people on the ramifications of violent crimes, teaching them how to grieve and process heartache. And yet in this moment, she was clueless to her own teachings, unable to see beyond her own immediate broken heart.

She reached for Felix's help, which wasn't easy. Her mother had given her plenty of couch sessions to retrain her brain to ask for help when she needed it.

And she needed it now.

Felix took her shaking hand and led her through the living room to the large glass door leading out to the deck overlooking the beach. When the glass slid open, the cool December air gently nudged them and Kelly took a long, deep breath and closed her watery eyes.

They sat on the deck furniture, close with their thighs touching, and Felix draped his arm around her shoulders. He was warm and firm and Kelly heaved a long sigh.

The beach was quiet, with a few lone joggers on the sand and a handful of surfers in the sea.

Kelly looked to the beautiful beach house next door. Her best friend Jill and her husband Nate lived there; two houses beyond that lived her other best friend Matt and his boyfriend Casey. They'd all known Overstreet too; he'd saved their lives . . . and Kelly had no fucking idea how to break this news to them.

"Don't worry," Felix said, intuitive as always. "I'll tell the others."

Kelly watched the waves lap the shore, the sun sparkling off the water. She loved living at the beach. She loved the ocean. She loved this *house*. She felt safe here, safe enough to hear the truth.

"Tell me what happened," she said, still holding Felix's hand.

Felix kissed her knuckles and said, "I was only given a preliminary report. He was discovered by garbage collectors near the RenCen at six-thirty this morning, Detroit time. They're still processing the scene. They waited to call me until they knew more."

"Tell me about *him*."

"He was wearing blue jeans, a blue-checked dress shirt, and a leather jacket. His badge was found in a jacket pocket, but his wallet wasn't. They've removed him from the scene. He's with the medical examiner now. Her name is Jessica. She's very good at her job. She'll treat him with respect."

"*And*?"

They watched seagulls fight over bread slices left by tourists, then Felix kissed Kelly's temple and said, "He was found in bad shape."

Kelly sucked in a breath, waiting for the rest.

Felix continued, "His hands and ankles were duct-taped together and his mouth was taped shut. Cause of death appears to be blunt force trauma to the back of the skull. Body temp suggests he'd only been dead a few hours when he was found. We won't know anymore until Jessica's finished with her initial report. She'll call me when it's ready."

Kelly squeezed Felix's fingers. Maybe if she transferred some of her pain onto him, she wouldn't hurt as much. It didn't work.

"Are there any leads?" she asked. "Suspects? *Anything*?"

"You don't have to worry about that," Felix said. "We're working on it. This is our top priority."

"I want to help. I *have* to. What can I do?"

Keeping herself occupied had always been Kelly's best defense—along with razor-sharp sarcasm—against emotion. Focusing on immediate action and strategy kept her from falling into despair. She'd done it in 1996 after her friends' killing spree, and again after Ford had died and Jill and Matt had gone to jail for one year; she'd researched and written her book to keep focus on anything but her grief.

"Actually, there is something you need to do," Felix said.

Kelly raised her head off his shoulder and looked in his eyes. He rarely told her to do anything—no one did—and it surprised her.

"What is it?" she asked.

Felix swallowed. "You need to go to Detroit to identify his body."

Kelly's chest seized like she'd been body-slammed by Hulk Hogan in the old videotapes Ford and Matt had watched as kids.

"*What*?" she asked.

"Kelly—"

"He was with the FBI for a hundred years. Everyone in Detroit knows what he looks like. They don't need *me* to tell them he's him."

"It's procedure, Kelly. His body has to be identified and confirmed by his next of kin, as well as sign for his personal effects."

"Then why don't they call Diane?"

"She's not his next of kin."

"Since when? She's his ex-wife. She's all the family he had."

Felix stared at her.

Fresh tears flooded Kelly's eyes.

She didn't need Sherlock Holmes to connect these dots.

"Tell me he didn't," she said. She and Overstreet had loved each other and been great friends, but surely he hadn't loved her so much to list her as his number one.

But Felix said, "You're listed as his next of kin in his official file."

"*Why*?"

"*You* were his family, Kelly."

Suddenly, all at once, Kelly felt important and appreciated and loved . . . and deeply, painfully sad.

She hugged Felix close.

He kissed her neck and stroked her hair and held on tight.

She sobbed into his T-shirt sleeve.

The seagulls squawked over the last breadcrumb.

The waves lapped the shore.

"I don't think I can," Kelly said, her voice muffled by Felix's bicep. "Identify his body? Nobody should have to do that."

"You're right. They shouldn't," Felix agreed. "But you do."

Kelly had only seen dead bodies at funerals, after they'd been made-up and polished and presented to the mourners as the prettiest versions possible. She'd never had to *identify* Mason or Ford or Berger immediately after they'd been killed, but now she was Overstreet's number one and she'd have to see what had happened to him.

She wasn't sure what identifying a body would even entail. Sure, she'd seen enough chilling episodes of *Law & Order* and *CSI* where a body was black-bagged on a metal table or rolled out of a freezer, but this wasn't a crime-show marathon.

This was real.

This was *Overstreet*.

Felix hugged her again and said, "You won't have to do it alone. I'll go with you."

Kelly nodded.

And as if reading her mind, Felix added, "You'll identify him from a photograph. You won't have to see him on a table or in a body bag like in the movies. I promise."

Kelly released a very slow sigh.

Any minute now, her instincts would reignite and she'd warp back into Wonder Woman, complete with straight posture, a confident gaze, great breasts, and unwavering nerves of steel, like she always did when it was needed or expected of her.

But for now, until it was necessary to kick the world's ass again, she held onto Felix.

And cried.

Because it mattered.

KELLY
7:56 AM PST

A soft tapping awoke Kelly. She checked the clock, but wasn't sure what time she'd fallen asleep. For a moment—a split second—she wondered why she was in bed at all.

Then she remembered: *Overstreet is dead.*

She'd crawled into bed after talking to Felix, exhausted from crying and remembering and wishing things were different. And while he'd made travel plans back to Detroit, Kelly had fallen asleep.

She wasn't sure how she'd lost so many hours so quickly, but the body—and its grief—always took what it needed to protect itself. Kelly had learned that too many times before.

Her eyes hurt from crying.

Her throat was terribly dry.

There were two more knocks and the bedroom door opened slowly. Standing on the other side was her best friend Jill, holding a glass of water and a small plate with two pain killers and a glazed donut.

Jill looked radiant, her porcelain skin and long blonde hair and casual white T-shirt almost luminescent in the dim light. Jill had been pretty since childhood, but as they approached thirty and benefitted from life's lessons, both young women had grown beyond pretty and become beautiful, in every sense.

Kelly wasn't surprised to see her. With a rock-solid twenty-five year friendship, they always just *knew* what the other needed.

And Kelly didn't realize how hungry she was until she saw the mouthwatering donut.

Jill set the glass and plate on the bedside table. She kissed Kelly's cheek and whispered, "Hey."

"Was it a dream?" Kelly asked, even though she knew it wasn't.

Jill shook her head and pushed a button on the wall beside the bed and the blackout blinds rose quietly. The sun had set but the moonlight and white stars pinpricking the evening sky gave the bedroom a warm glow.

Kelly sat up, resting her back against the headboard.

Jill sat beside her and combed Kelly's hair out of her face.

"Felix told me what happened," Jill said softly.

Kelly held Jill's hand close to her chest.

"I'm so sorry, Kelly."

Jill's words held more than support. She knew what Kelly and Overstreet had meant to each other, having witnessed their friendship deepen over many years. But Jill was personally involved and held a lot of love for the fallen FBI agent too.

"He's dead, Jill," Kelly whispered. "*Our* Overstreet. *Dead*."

Jill nodded. "I know."

"He was just here a week ago. A fucking *week*. He was thanking us for inviting him to another California Thanksgiving with our Island of Misfit Toys, and now he's—"

"Kelly, I *know*."

Kelly wiped her face and flipped her hair, desperate for her strong façade—the Kelly Spencer she presented to the world—to reappear.

"I'm not going to say it's not fair," she said. "We've lived too much life and been through too much to know that life is never fair, *but*—"

"It's not fucking fair," Jill said with a defeated smile.

"It's fucking *not*! I wasn't done with him yet."

They laughed, but only for a moment. When it waned and settled until the room was silent, they held hands and their eyes watered, but they didn't cry. They'd done enough of that for now.

"I have to . . . *identify* him," Kelly said, unblinking.

Jill nodded like she already knew—Felix had probably told her—and said, "Matty and I will go with you."

Kelly shook her head. "Felix is going with me. You and Matty shouldn't have to go through it too."

"You sure? You know I don't mind."

"I know. I'll call you if I need you."

"You better," Jill said. "Felix said you leave in the morning, *early*."

Kelly rubbed her eyes. "I have a lot of shit to do then. I have to pack and call Diane and—"

"I'll do that."

"Will you call the schools too? I'm speaking at three high schools and four colleges next week."

"I'll take care of it."

"It's ironic, huh? I'm supposed to educate them on the aftermath of violence and I have to cancel because my friend was murdered."

Kelly's breath caught in her dry throat and she covered her mouth with both hands to keep anymore wounded cries from escaping.

Jill handed Kelly the painkillers and water glass.

Kelly popped the pills and drank the entire glass without stopping.

"Just *rest*," Jill said. "I'll take care of all that shit."

Kelly took a breath and nodded. "Thank you."

Jill handed her the donut next. Kelly took a large bite. It was sugary and sweet and *delicious* and for a second, she felt like herself again. Fuck, she loved carbs!

Jill kissed Kelly's cheek again and hugged her.

Earlier on the deck with Felix, Kelly had felt safe with him. She felt it again now, in Jill's arms; safe, yet desperately unsure of whatever the hell came next.

Jill smiled like she recognized something in Kelly's eyes and said, "You'll survive this, Kelly. You've done it before. We both have."

Kelly believed her, because she knew it to be true.

She *had* survived this before—loss and pain and debilitating grief.

That didn't make it any easier or hurt less, but it gave her hope.

She'd survive this.

Again.

KELLY

SATURDAY, DECEMBER 3, 2005
10:26 AM EST

Kelly had insisted she and Felix go straight to the medical examiner's office after landing in Detroit. She didn't want to check into a hotel or visit Overstreet's ex-wife or any old haunts or get on with life yet.

She couldn't.

She needed to identify Overstreet's body first.

And get it over with as soon as humanly possible.

Felix had been the doting, supportive boyfriend during the flight—keeping Kelly fed and hydrated and comfortable—but also allowing large chunks of silence to exist between them. Kelly didn't want to talk—not yet—and Felix respected her need to be withdrawn. Her guns would eventually blaze, but for now she wanted to be quiet and grieve and learn everything she could.

After watching their every step through the icy sidewalks and sky-high snowbanks—and remembering how much they hated Michigan winters—Kelly and Felix were greeted in the Wayne County Building foyer by a tall heavily-pregnant woman with beautiful brown skin, a dazzling smile and wild long black curls. But all Kelly noticed were the file folders tucked under her arm, presumably stuffed to the brim with information and reports and *photographs* of Overstreet.

Overstreet is dead.

Kelly's chest seized and she swallowed hard, refusing to puke all over the beautifully-polished granite foyer flooring.

The woman shook Felix's hand. "It's nice to see you again, Felix."

"You too." Felix looked at Kelly and added, "This is Kelly Spencer."

"Hello, Ms. Spencer. I'm Jessica Gentry, the medical examiner who cared for Frank Overstreet." She shook Kelly's hand.

"Call me Kelly, please."

Jessica smelled like vanilla and chai spice and Kelly appreciated her firm handshake, a sign of respect Grandmother Rose had taught her as a child. She'd firmly shaken every hand since.

"Felix told me a lot about you," Jessica added. "You're the envy of a lot of women around here and mailroom Kyle. Felix is quite the catch."

Kelly cracked a smile. "Congratulations," she said, nodding to Jessica's stomach. "When are you due?"

"Ugh! Christmas Day. Finally!" Jessica cheered. "I'm ready. This kid has tap-danced on my bladder enough."

"How's Bill?" Felix asked. "Excited?"

"Are you kidding? He's already baby-proofed our house. I can't get into my own medicine cabinet or the laundry room."

Kelly appreciated Jessica's small talk too, attempting to make the situation as comfortable as possible. But knowing she'd *see* Overstreet's body and face soon, no amount of lighthearted pleasantries would delay the inevitable or slow her racing heart.

They rode the elevator to the second floor while an ill-timed muzak version of *We'll Meet Again* played on the overhead speakers.

Kelly clutched Felix's hand as they followed Jessica down a busy aisle of cubicles. Keyboard strokes and telephone calls and chitchat congested the already-warm air. Kelly was on edge and wasn't sure she could take so much distraction.

But then Jessica opened a thick wooden door and the three of them entered an office oasis—quiet, low lighting, with a large table and four comfortable leather chairs, a credenza stuffed with refreshments, even a small radio playing jazz at very low volume—no medical tables or spooky blue lighting or body bags or a toe tags in sight.

"Would you like something to drink or eat?" Jessica asked.

Kelly stared at the credenza, loaded with bottled drinks, ripe fruit and trail mix. She wasn't sure who the hell would eat a fucking apple in this situation, but she gulped water when Jessica handed her a bottle.

"Please, have a seat." Jessica motioned to the leather-upholstered chairs. She placed the small stack of folders on the tabletop and sat.

Felix sat across from her and Kelly sat beside him.

Kelly never took her eyes off the folders.

"I'm going to show you three photographs, Kelly," Jessica said. "One close-up of the face, one headshot, and one profile. The face has suffered significant damage, but has been cleaned. He was found with duct tape over his mouth, but that has been removed. You will not see tape or blood, but there are significant contusions and bruising."

Jessica's tone was calm and caring, and her S's were whispery yet sharp, almost singsongy. Kelly wondered how many times Jessica had given this same speech, how many parents and lovers and kids had sat in these lush leather chairs and identified their dead loved ones.

But Kelly sensed Jessica gave a damn, that this was more than science or work for her, that she cared for the people she examined. Felix had promised Jessica would treat Overstreet's body with respect. Kelly fully believed him now.

"If at any time you need a break or you have a question, just let me know," Jessica said. "We're not in a rush. Take your time."

She opened the file . . .

And Kelly covered her mouth with both hands.

Staring up at her from the muted-white folder was a close-up color photograph of Frank Overstreet's eyes, nose and mouth. He was pale, but handsome. His eyes were closed, his eyelashes long and black, his hair short and more salt than pepper. He'd jokingly blamed Kelly and her friends for accelerating his graying, but he'd always looked so sophisticated with it.

There was reddening and swelling around his chapped mouth, from duct tape Kelly assumed, but there were no other signs of trauma.

But when Jessica flipped to the next photograph—a wider headshot with ears, neck and shoulders—Kelly saw pure destruction.

There was a long, deep laceration from Overstreet's hairline, down his temple to just above his left ear, and dark purple-blue bruising and scrapes on his neck and right shoulder.

Tears suddenly blurred Kelly's vision.

Felix handed her a tissue and she wiped her eyes.

In 1999, Kelly had painted Overstreet's face with fake bruises and cuts for a zombie-themed New Year's Eve party at Nate's bar The Crabby Cabana. He'd looked eerily similar to these photographs.

But these weren't play wounds for a shitty Venice Beach bar party.

These were real, and fatal, and on her friend.

The third photograph—a profile of the left side of Overstreet's head, with a large chunk of his skull and hair missing just above and behind the ear, the hole large and missing both bone *and* brains—made Kelly leap out of her chair and puke into a eucalyptus-scented trashcan near the beautifully-ripened fruit. The orange juice and blueberry muffin she'd eaten on the plane splashed into the trash.

Felix knelt beside her, holding her shiny dark hair in one hand and rubbing her back with the other.

"Do you want to stop, Kelly?" Jessica asked.

"No." Kelly stood and swished her mouth with water. "I'm sorry."

"Don't apologize. That trashcan has seen a lot of that." Jessica flashed a tiny, encouraging smile.

"Are you okay?" Felix asked, his face focused and concerned.

Kelly held his hand and nodded. "I'm okay."

They retook their seats.

Kelly inhaled deeply, exhaled slowly, and looked at the third photograph—and Overstreet's horrific injuries—again.

While researching her book, Kelly had avoided the explicit autopsy photos of her friend Ford, their bully Mason and his co-killer Berger. She hadn't wanted to see an exploded ribcage or a skull crushed by a refrigerator door or a jawbone blown off with a stolen shotgun. She wanted to remember them young and healthy and *alive*.

And yet now, in this warm, well-scented, low-jazzed office, Kelly's last images that would influence her memory of her wonderful friend Overstreet were from his autopsy.

"What happened to him?" Kelly's voice was quiet but determined.

Jessica spoke softly too, and slowly, as if to ensure Kelly paid attention to every detail, "He was struck in the head with a heavy metal object, probably a crowbar or a tire iron. It shattered the piece of his skull you see in the third photograph. He was hit again on the opposite side as well, near the hairline, as you see in the second photograph."

Tears fell from Kelly's eyes and splashed onto Felix's knuckles. He moved his chair closer to her and put his free hand on her back.

"Kelly, can you confirm this is Frank Overstreet?" Jessica asked.

Kelly nodded.

"I'm sorry, Kelly. I need you to vocally confirm it."

Kelly wiped her face. "Yes. That's Frank Overstreet."

Jessica smiled weakly, like she understood and respected Kelly's pain, and closed the folder, covering Overstreet's face. She wrote a few notes, then slid a document across the table with a pen and said, "I'll need your signature on this confirmation."

Kelly signed it and Jessica put it in a separate folder.

"His body will be held temporarily during the initial investigation," Jessica said. "Then he will be released to you as his next of kin. But I will help you with funeral home transfers or cremation or whatever you need, when you're ready."

Kelly nodded, but she wasn't really listening.

She couldn't stop thinking about her friend's permanently-closed eyes, or his prickly five o'clock shadow that would never again see a razor, or . . . the gaping empty hole in the side of his head.

Kelly coughed away the fiery lump in her throat. "Did he suffer?"

Jessica laced her fingers together. "I don't like the word *suffer*; too many interpretations. But in this case Frank Overstreet was a *fighter*. His wounds are consistent with self-defense, a fighter's injuries."

Kelly knew Overstreet was tough and she appreciated Jessica's attempt at helping Kelly hold onto the memory of that strength, but Kelly wasn't satisfied. She wanted the truth.

"If you're asking if he died quickly," Jessica added. "The answer is no. His injuries were very painful and he died slowly."

That was the goddamn definition of suffering, but Kelly didn't give impromptu grammar lessons. She was too tired to lash out.

"Do you have any more questions?" Jessica asked.

Kelly had a lot of fucking questions.

Like, why the hell was her friend dead?

Or, who the hell did this?

Or, why the fuck did the trashcan smell like eucalyptus?

But she couldn't voice any of those questions, not here, not to a medical examiner. She needed to think and organize her thoughts before she could consider what came next.

So she whispered to Jessica, "Thank you for taking care of him."

"You're welcome, Kelly."

The walls felt restrictive, as if inching closer, trying to squash Kelly alive. She looked at Felix and asked, "Can we get out of here, please?"

Felix didn't ask questions or console her. Instead, he stood, pulled out her chair and grabbed their jackets.

"Jessica, thank you," he said and opened the door. "I'll call you if we have any questions."

Kelly left the room and Felix quickly followed, having to take large steps to keep up with her.

They rode the elevator back to the foyer.

Felix helped Kelly put on her last-minute airport-purchased winter jacket and just before they hit the front doors to enter the brutal Michigan winter, a voice called to them from behind.

"Excuse me!"

They turned to see a man hustling toward them from the security desk. He looked like an extra from *Revenge of the Nerds*—young, pimpled, pocket-protector, probably fresh out of college.

"Kelly Spencer?" he asked and pushed his glasses up the bridge his nose. Kelly hadn't seen nerds actually do that since the *Leave It to Beaver* reruns she'd watched as a child.

"Yes, I'm Kelly Spencer."

"I'm sorry for your loss and I apologize for my poor timing."

"Who are you?" Felix asked, protectively keeping his hand on Kelly's back. "How did you find us here?"

"Special Agent Macallum, I presume? Your office told me you'd be here. My name is Edward Andrews. I'm a will and probate attorney with the bureau." He handed Kelly a large envelope with her name and address printed on a glossy white label on the front. "This is a copy of Special Agent Frank Overstreet's last will and testament."

Kelly took the envelope. It was thick and heavy and she gave it to Felix to carry. She was tired and couldn't be bothered by its contents or this conversation.

But she still asked, "Why do I need this?"

Andrews seemed surprised, looking at both of them with wide eyes. "I assumed you knew," he said. "You're Overstreet's benefactor."

"*What*?"

"He's left everything to you, Ms. Spencer, including his pension."

Kelly didn't understand.

She was Overstreet's next of kin *and* his benefactor?

Overstreet had been smart with money and worth quite a bit of it. Kelly knew he'd invested heavily in eighties tech companies and the stock market, but now all that hard work—his three decades with the FBI and smart investments and economic brilliance—was hers?

She was embarrassed.

She hadn't earned such a gift and didn't deserve it.

Why hadn't he left it to Diane, his ex-wife and close friend?

"If you have any questions, my information is inside the envelope," Andrews said. "Again, I'm very sorry for your loss. Frank Overstreet was a wonderful man."

He left and Kelly stood in the foyer, her arms hanging heavy at her side. She was just so tired. She'd processed way too much information in less than two days.

"Are you okay?" Felix asked again.

Kelly wasn't really sure what she was. She wasn't *okay*, but she'd survived the identification, like she knew she would. She'd read Overstreet's will at some point, and survive that too. But for now she needed fresh air, even bitter-cold December Michigan air.

"Do you want to go to Dutch Girl Donuts?" Felix offered. "I'll let you eat as many carbs as you want."

Kelly smiled.

Goddamn this guy knew her.

And *holy shit* was she dependant on donuts in times of crisis.

She held his hand again, kissed his knuckles, and said, "*Yes*."

KELLY

1: 15 PM EST

When Diane Overstreet opened the front door to her home, she greeted Kelly with a bright smile, the kind that made her eyes squint and almost disappear. Dressed in a festive Christmas sweater, Diane was small, just under five feet and many inches shorter than Kelly, with a chubby-cheeked face and short red-rinsed hair. She was early-sixties but often mistaken for much younger, vibrant and joyful and full of life.

But on the snowy front porch of her Grosse Pointe Park home, her usually lively face was sullen, the smile fake and forced.

She hugged Kelly, gently patting her back. "How are you holding up?" she asked, her voice high and squeaky. Overstreet had always called her his Betty Boop.

"I'm okay," Kelly lied. "You?"

Diane smiled again, this time with an understanding edge, as if she too was doing as well as she could.

She looked at Felix and playfully pointed to her left cheek. He laughed and kissed it.

"Thanks for coming. I wasn't sure you'd be up to it, but it' so good to see you both, given the circumstances," she said. "Come on in. I'll make a fresh pot of thick-black coffee, just the way you both like it."

Diane waved to the not-so-undercover FBI agent sitting in a black car across the street—her newly-appointed security detail, just in case Overstreet's killer targeted his family and friends next.

Kelly and Felix removed their winter wear and relaxed in the home's almost-too-hot interior. A small Christmas tree twinkled in the living room and the house smelled like baked apples and cinnamon.

Felix excused himself to the study, claiming he had telephone calls to make, although Kelly knew he was giving her and Diane privacy.

While Diane made coffee, Kelly sat in the heavily-picture-framed living room. There were childhood photographs of Diane and Overstreet's son David, who'd been killed in a convenience store robbery in the nineties. Their marriage hadn't survived his death, although they'd remained very close friends. So close in fact, that two framed photographs of their wedding day sat on the fireplace mantel, beside David's high school graduation photo.

Kelly respected Diane's never-ending support of Overstreet, having helped him through many difficult cases over the years. Kelly invited Diane to every holiday celebration over the years and Diane had accepted a few. There was even a framed photograph of the three of them together on Kelly's deck taken last Christmas.

Diane set a serving tray on the dining room table, with drinks and holiday-colored Oreo cookies. Overstreet had always praised her ability to entertain. The table was even covered in a colorful Christmas cloth with dancing reindeer and Ol' Saint Nick in his sleigh.

Kelly joined her, sitting near the bright windows overlooking the large snowy backyard. She took the steaming cup of coffee, sipped, and asked, "Did you know I was his next of kin and benefactor?"

Diane sat poised with her hands folded in her lap. "He declared that two years ago, when he finally decided to retire. He wanted everything in order, even though he never retired." She giggled a little, as if the very thought of Overstreet retiring was absurd.

"Two *years* ago?" Kelly asked, almost hurt, like she couldn't be trusted with something so important. "Why didn't he tell me?"

"That wasn't his style, you know that." Diane sipped green tea with milk and one sugar cube. "He knew it would embarrass you and you'd try to talk him out of it."

"It does and I would've! I don't want this responsibility."

"Yes, you do. You're *you*. You'll take the responsibility because there's no way you'd let anyone else have it."

Kelly tilted her head and smirked.

Diane knew her shit.

Kelly wouldn't want someone else having any piece of Overstreet. He was *hers* and she was protective. But she couldn't shake the confusion of *why*; why had Overstreet chosen her? Too many goddamn *whys*.

Diane seemed to sense Kelly's internal struggle. She set down her tea cup—making a delicately soft *clink*—and leaned across the table and playfully pinched Kelly's wrist.

"Frank always said you were the human form of joy," Diane said. "You make people laugh and feel special and understood. You bring *joy*. That's why you're his benefactor. You were a great friend to him.

He loved you not like a daughter or an acquaintance or any of the past survivors he'd kept in touch with, but like a *friend*. An equal."

Kelly wasn't sure what to say to that. She knew Overstreet had respected her, but she wasn't prepared for Diane to pull back the curtain to reveal Overstreet's deep admiration and love. And her throat was tight, but she wasn't sure she had anymore tears left to cry.

"But his *benefactor*? It's probably a lot of money."

"It is," Diane agreed. "So what?"

"But—"

Diane smiled, as if one step ahead as usual. "Don't worry about me. Frank made sure I'm taken care of too." She laughed, shook her head, and added, "He never knew how to tell us he loved us while he was alive, so this is his way of telling us after he's gone."

"I don't need it," Kelly said, defiantly.

"You're young. Of course you do."

"It's too much. I made more than I'll ever need off my book."

"Then do something with it. Pay off that ridiculously-beautiful house you have or travel the world for the rest of your life or use it to marry that handsome FBI agent who loves you."

Kelly rolled her eyes. Overstreet had pressured her to marry Felix enough; she didn't need it from his ex-wife too.

"Just make Frank proud and be happy," Diane added. "That's all he'd want from you."

"I will," Kelly promised and meant it.

"Good." Diane smoothed a small wrinkle in the tablecloth. "Now, there's something else."

Kelly groaned. "I hate when there's something else."

"I know. I sound like Frank. But this is important."

Diane went to a small closet near the front door and returned with a large cardboard archive box. Dozens of words and numbers that meant nothing to Kelly were scribbled on each side in thick black marker, its lid sealed with dark-red tape.

Diane set the box on top of tablecloth-Santa and stood near it, not next to it, like she was uncomfortable—or scared—of its contents.

"What's that?" Kelly asked.

Diane shrugged awkwardly, as if unsure of where to begin.

"Diane?"

Diane motioned to the box with both hands, as if she were modeling the next item up for bids on *The Price is Right*, and said, "Frank left instructions to give this to you in the event of his death."

"What is this, *Ghost*?" Kelly laughed. "Is he going to send messages through Whoopi Goldberg and slide pennies under the door?"

Diane didn't share Kelly's laughter. "His lawyer delivered it yesterday. Frank knew I would get it to you."

Kelly's smile dropped. "You're serious?"

Diane nodded.

Kelly stood from the table and studied the box's top.

Written in thick black letters were three names:

FAWN ELIZABETH SCHULTZ
JAMES WILLIAM BERGER
GRANT THEODORE CARVER

Kelly looked back to Diane and asked, "What is this?"

"A decade's obsession." Diane folded her arms across her holiday sweater, her still-worn wedding ring sparkling against its soft red threads. "That's everything Frank had on your friends Fawn and Berger and . . . Grant Carver."

"Who the hell is Grant Carver?"

"The one who got away."

"What does that mean?"

Diane sat down, keeping her teary face away from Kelly.

"Diane?" Kelly had never seen Diane cry in all the years she'd known her. It alarmed her. The unknown Grant Carver was obviously vital to whatever story Kelly had yet to read.

Diane wouldn't look at her. She stared at the large fluffy snowflakes falling outside the dining room windows.

"Felix!" Kelly shouted.

Seconds later, he rushed in. "What is it? Are you okay?"

"Who's Grant Carver?"

Felix was stoic, looking at Diane, then Kelly, but said nothing.

"Will one of you tell me what the hell's going on?" Kelly urged.

Slowly, Diane turned toward them, her teary eyes landing on Felix first. She dabbed her face with a tissue from inside her sweater sleeve and nodded to him, as if she couldn't speak or give a calm explanation.

Finally, Felix said, "He's a killer, Kelly."

Kelly wasn't satisfied.

There was something else; she *knew* it.

Overstreet had once complimented her fine-tuned intuition.

That intuition was roaring now.

"*Overstreet's* killer?" she asked.

Diane released a small, pained whimper.

And Felix softly said, "*Yes.*"

He'd told Kelly that Overstreet's murder matched a killer's M.O.

Those methods were Grant Carver's?

Kelly pointed to the box top names. "Overstreet knew him?"

"He'd been investigating him for a decade," Felix said.

Overstreet had shared a lot of work stories with Kelly, but she couldn't remember a Grant Carver or any specifics on an active serial killer. Why hadn't Overstreet mentioned him?

Then Kelly saw the box top again and asked, "What the hell does he have to do with Berger and Fawn?"

Felix took a breath, as if allowing any dust to settle before telling Kelly anything else.

Diane stood again, her head high as if to force courage, and gave Felix a confident nod, encouraging him to continue.

So Felix said, "Overstreet suspected Grant was linked to them somehow. He always thought there was more to Fawn's story. Whether he figured it out or not, I don't know."

"What's in the box?" Kelly asked, cautiously pointing to it like it might explode at any moment.

"Everything he has on all of them."

"Why didn't he tell me about this?"

Before Felix could answer, Diane said, "Kelly, you are . . . *sensitive* when it comes to Berger and Fawn, understandably so. Frank didn't want to upset you with any ideas or hunches about them that might've turned out to be nothing. They've hurt you enough. Frank didn't want to hurt you anymore."

"So he drops his unfinished life's work in my lap after he's dead?" Kelly snapped with a frustrated laugh. "What am I supposed to do with whatever's in this box?"

Diane forced a smile. "Maybe it's the recipe to solve another great mystery, Nancy Drew."

Kelly dug her fingernail into the box's red tape, wondering not only what was in it, but why the hell it was now her responsibility.

But like being declared Overstreet's benefactor, Kelly knew he'd trusted her and he'd known she'd fight and claw and do whatever necessary to follow through on the box's contents.

"That motherfucker!" she playfully snapped.

They all managed a laugh, loud and giggly and needed.

Then the room fell painfully silent.

Kelly couldn't take her eyes off the box.

Diane cleared her throat and offered, "You can stay here if you want, make the dining room your base of operations."

"I'll take it to my mother's house," Kelly said, "I feel safer there, if that makes sense."

Diane hugged her. "Makes perfect sense."

"I can't let this go, Diane. Whether it's Grant Carver or someone else, I have to catch him."

Diane rubbed Kelly's cheek and whispered, "You will."

Kelly's limbs stared to shake with adrenaline.

She wanted to know more.

She wanted to know *everything*.

Who the fuck was Grant Carver?

"We have to go," Kelly said to Felix and grabbed the box off the tabletop. It was much heavier than she'd expected and it fell back onto the tabletop with a thunderous BANG! She gripped harder and yanked.

"Thank you," Kelly said and kissed Diane's cheek.

"Before you go—" Diane said carefully. "Do you want to talk about the funeral?"

Kelly's heart jackhammered her chest.

She hadn't thought of that.

Overstreet needed a funeral.

Overstreet is dead.

Kelly had never planned a funeral, but she'd seen the stress and pain they'd caused the deads' family and friends.

Kelly wasn't sure she had it in her.

Diane smiled softly, as if sensing Kelly's discomfort, and said, "I'll help you." A big tear—the crocodile kind grandmothers always talked about—rolled down her left cheek.

Kelly nodded.

She needed to catch a killer before she could talk caskets.

She inhaled a sharp breath and said, "I have to see this through before I can let myself think about that."

Diane smiled again, proudly, as if she knew Kelly's plan without words. She'd been married to Overstreet. Maybe she recognized some of his tenacity and strong-will in Kelly.

"His body will be held for a while," Diane said. "We'll talk later."

Kelly kissed her again, as did Felix.

Then Kelly held the box—Overstreet's potential legacy—and left.

Her guns were blazing now.

And she was *ready*.

KELLY
3:37 PM EST

Kelly's mother Linda was on her yearly singles cruise in the Bahamas with her psychiatric coworker colleagues, so the usually-jovial house was very quiet and still when Kelly and Felix arrived.

Kelly and her mother had been a powerhouse dynamic duo since 1987, after Kelly's father attacked Linda on one last alcoholic bender and went to jail, then disappeared. They had a great relationship, but Kelly was happy not having to answer any of her mother's patented introspective or probing questions.

The house hadn't changed much since Kelly's childhood, but Linda had redecorated Kelly's bedroom shortly after she'd moved to California in 1997. Still, whenever Kelly entered it, she remembered the Luke Perry and Christian Slater posters on the walls, the pink Casio boombox blaring Debbie Gibson and Janet Jackson cassette tapes, the New Kids on the Block bedsheets, and the slumber parties with Jill and Fawn from her youth.

The room was now painted in dark greens and burgundies, with a large guest bed covered in overstuffed cushions, and smelled like linen-scented candles, a far cry from pre-teen Kelly's *Electric Youth* perfume.

Kelly set Overstreet's archive box on the bed. The mattress was firm and took the weight of it, although Kelly half-expected the bed to collapse, as if the box's contents could destroy anything it touched.

"Do you need any help?" Felix asked, standing in the doorway.

Kelly smiled at him. She felt safe with him there, not only because he was strong and a highly-trained field agent, but because he understood her better than most. And he'd tell her the truth, no matter how nervous she was to proceed or how scary the answer.

So Kelly took a breath and said, "Tell me about Grant Carver."

Felix leaned against the doorframe and folded his arms across his chest. "Are you sure you want to know?"

"I'm about to open Pandora's Box. I'd rather you soften its blow."

"This doesn't have to be your fight, Kelly."

"It already is."

Felix nodded, a nonverbal agreement to help her anyway she needed, and said, "Grant Carver is a man the FBI has been chasing for over a decade. In 1995, he killed his father and surrendered shortly after, but it was declared self-defense and he was released without charge. He disappeared the day after, but the killing continued. He went dormant for ten years, then resurfaced six months ago at his ten-year high school reunion here in Michigan."

Kelly appreciated Felix not tiptoeing around her and getting straight to specifics. She wanted—*needed*—to know everything, even the ugly parts, if she hoped to catch the bastard who'd killed her friend.

"Why did he resurface?" Kelly asked.

"To see an old boyfriend," Felix said.

"Who's the boyfriend?"

"Oliver Foster."

"Why do I know that name?"

"Oliver is the man who jumped to his death from the Marina del Rey apartment balcony six months ago. He was trying to escape Grant. It was Overstreet's last case."

"*That* was Oliver and Grant?"

Felix nodded.

Marina del Rey was only twenty or so miles from Kelly's house and she remembered the news reports. Oliver had survived the initial jump, but he'd later died in the hospital from catastrophic injuries.

"Oliver's friend, a woman named Char Wolff, was on the telephone with him when he jumped," Felix added. "She'd just told him the truth to Grant's crimes. Oliver feared for his life and, as Char said, he couldn't emotionally handle the revelation that the love of his life was a serial killer. So, he . . . *jumped*."

Kelly's heart seized like her memories were choke-holding it, trying to squeeze the life out of whatever strength she had left.

Because she certainly knew a thing or two about deceit and painful revelations and loving the wrong people. In 1996, her childhood friend Fawn claimed she'd been brutally raped by their senior classmate Mason Strauss. Kelly's closest friends—Berger, Ford, Matt and Jill—retaliated against Mason, attacking him in his own home. He'd later died from the injuries they'd caused.

Or so they thought.

After the near-death of a convenience store clerk and two more horrific deaths, the truth came out that Fawn had orchestrated an elaborate lie, manipulating the others into believing they'd killed Mason, initially with Berger's enthusiastic help, when the reality was Fawn and Berger alone had killed Mason, returning to his home after the initial attack and using the refrigerator door to smash his skull.

But fiercely-devoted friends Jill, Matt and Ford had hit the open road with the well-concealed killers, oblivious to the truth, to escape authorities, hiding out in the middle-of-nowhere Fontaine Motel, which later lit up like the Fourth of July in gunfire, Fawn and Berger against the FBI and the Oklahoma State Police. Fawn was apprehended, but not before blasting Ford in the back and Berger in the face with a stolen twelve-gauge shotgun.

Mason, Berger and Ford had died before Fawn's true identity—as a meek and mild maniac—had been revealed, so Kelly felt immediate compassion for Oliver Foster; she understood why he'd jumped. Some truths are too hard to hear. Kelly had barely survived the loss of Ford or the betrayal that her dear childhood friend had caused it.

But she'd fought for her survival and she'd devoted her life to helping others survive too. She'd never known Oliver, but wished she could've helped him too.

"We were *this close* to catching Grant at the apartment," Felix said, holding his thumb and index finger together. "But he escaped."

"Was Overstreet there?" Kelly asked.

"No. He was here in Michigan with Char. They didn't arrive until later that night, after Oliver died and Grant disappeared."

"Did Grant know Overstreet was investigating him?"

"He must have. Overstreet made the official announcement when Oliver died. He named Grant on the news and in all the papers."

Kelly inhaled a long, deep breath. "Did Grant kill Overstreet for revenge, blaming him for Oliver's death?"

"Maybe? We don't have a motive for any of his killings," Felix said.

"How many are there?"

"Seven that we can confirm, including Overstreet."

"How did you identify the other victims?"

"Char found a disposable camera in an old backpack belonging to Grant. It had photographs of his first three victims. Those victims' deaths match three others almost perfectly."

"How?"

"Grant's method is distinct. His murder weapon is opportunistic; he grabs whatever's available, like a bottle or a telephone. But he uses duct tape in such a way that is distinctly his. A lot of killers use duct tape, even Berger and Fawn used it, but no known killer ties impecca-bly-formed bowties on their victims' ankles and wrists with it, except Grant. That detail was never made public, so it couldn't have been a copycat, and too specific to be random."

"Did Overstreet have the same bowties?"

Felix paused, then gently said, "*Yes*."

Kelly sucked in a breath.

The bowties matched.

Grant's distinct calling card.

Grant Carver had killed Frank Overstreet.

"How the hell do you make a bowtie out of duct tape?" she asked.

Felix shrugged. "Patience? It can't be easy, but it's meticulous."

"Did you work the case after Oliver jumped?"

"Overstreet handed the case to my department after he returned to Michigan." Felix paused, as if searching for delicate words. "He was really . . . *sad* when Oliver died, like he could have or *should* have done more to save him. He didn't have it in him to keep chasing a ghost."

"Why didn't either of you tell me about it?"

"Like Diane said, you're sensitive when it comes to hard cases, es-pecially murder cases, and I work a lot of them. I don't want to tell you about all the death I see every day. It's not something I want you to carry. I'm sure it was the same for Overstreet."

Kelly smiled at Felix's sincerity and protective instincts. And she understood. At the time, Grant's case was just another killer, another chase, another case. No one knew it would end in Overstreet's death; no one except Overstreet himself, if the notes on his box were any clue.

The box.

Fawn, Berger *and* Grant's names were on it.

"What does Grant have to do with Berger and Fawn?" Kelly asked.

Felix shrugged. "Overstreet and I never talked about Berger and Fawn unless we were talking about your book. He once told me there might be more to the story, but he never shared any theories."

Kelly stared at the box, her fingers itching to start.

"Do you want me to help you go through it?" Felix asked.

"No," Kelly said. "But will you stay close?"

"Of course. I'll be in the living room on my computer."

Kelly kissed him and closed the door after he left.

The bedroom was quiet—too quiet.

Kelly turned on the small beside radio, keeping its volume just enough to hear the dull hum of Heart's *Barracuda*, and sat on the bed.

Before she could second-guess or doubt herself, she sliced a nail file through the red tape sealing the archive box, and lifted its lid.

Inside were dozens of vertically-filed folders, intricately organized and labeled in Overstreet's easily-recognizable but hard-to-read left-handed scrawl or typed on fading white labels with an old typewriter.

Kelly did a quick flip through the folder tabs: CARVER CAMERA '95 to SCHULTZ REPORTS, FONTAINE FLOORPLANS to CARVER SIGHTINGS, OLIVER FOSTER to one marked simply CARVER.

She was instinctively drawn to the FONTAINE SNAPSHOTS folder. Inside, she found a large manila envelope labeled with her own name.

She instantly recognized it.

Overstreet had given it to her in 1996, after Fawn's full confession. Kelly's friends had documented their road trip with an instant camera and Overstreet had made copies of the snapshots for Kelly, but she'd refused them. She'd seen a few in Matt's hands—caked with Ford's blood—shortly after the shootout and they'd broken her heart; she'd refused to see any more.

But now, nine and a half years later, Kelly was ready.

She wanted to see them again, to see *Ford* again.

She opened the file and pulled out color photocopies of a dozen instant snapshots . . . and there they were, her friends, lively and eighteen again: Berger's round face and thick goatee; Jill's beautiful long blonde hair flying in the breeze as she laughed; Fawn hiding a giggle behind paint-chipped fingers; and Matt's goofy grin beside Ford's smoldering stare, both of them deeply in love with each other.

The snapshots showed them swimming in the Fontaine's pool and eating sandwiches and drinking beer and smoking cigarettes and living a blissfully ignorant life before the truth and death ruined everything.

Several of the snapshots' white strips were labeled in Ford's handwriting, like MY LI'L MARTIAN on an image of Matt and Ford or WEIRDOS on one of Jill, Matt and Ford together.

Kelly's chest ached. She missed her old life and these weirdos.

She was off track now, travelling down her own memory lane instead of focusing on Grant's, but she forgave herself. No one would know if she briefly lost herself or shed a few tears.

She'd never had unrestricted access to her friends' histories and detailed images before. She'd studied all the available police reports in researching her book, but this was different. She hadn't been brave enough to look at these snapshots then. Now, after nearly a decade's worth of clarity and healing, she was braver than she'd ever been.

Kelly left a photo of Jill, Matt and Ford together beside the pool on the bedside table, and returned the rest to the manila envelope.

And before she'd allow her heart to ache or tears to flow too badly, she opened the SCHULTZ REPORTS folder.

Inside were dozens of progress reports on Fawn—behavioral, medical, psychological, work history in the prison library and cafeteria. Most of the information bored Kelly—Fawn was a healthy twenty-seven year old woman, an avid book reader and letter writer, no remorse for her crimes, quiet and reserved but with frequent outbursts toward guards and fellow inmates.

Kelly wasn't surprised by the remorse or the outbursts. She'd spoken to enough witnesses from the Fontaine Motel shooting to know Fawn had hidden rage inside her, but the mention of letter writing peeked Kelly's interest.

Fawn is an avid letter writer, sending and receiving multiple letters every week.

Who the hell was sending Fawn letters?

The report mentioned a prison pen pal program, but Kelly wasn't convinced. Fawn had always been isolated and reserved and didn't make friends easily. Kelly couldn't imagine her now swapping recipes or crochet patterns with strangers. There had to be a reason, although with Fawn there'd never been any reasons.

After her arrest and conviction, Fawn had written Jill and Matt several letters. Matt returned them to the prison without ever opening them. Fawn had killed Ford—the love of Matt's life—and Matt wasn't interested in reading her words.

Jill never opened Fawn's letters either. Instead, she'd given them to Kelly to use as research for her book, although Kelly too never opened them. She'd stashed them in an old shoebox under her childhood bed and had left it behind when she'd moved out, refusing to travel cross country with a killer's letter.

Her childhood bed had sat in the same spot as the bed she sat on now, and Kelly had never thought of the letters until this moment.

She peeked under the bed—just in case—but there was no box or letters, just well-vacuumed carpet and an extra blanket.

Kelly pulled out her sleek Motorola Razr and dialed her mother.

Linda answered after two rings, "Kelly! My baby!"

Kelly heard clinking glasses and laughter and *life* on the line. Kelly hadn't told her mother about Overstreet's death because she knew Linda would race back to be with her. Kelly didn't need that yet.

Kelly smiled and said, "Are you drunk, Mom?"

"Of course I'm drunk!" Linda cheered. "The margaritas are *freeee!*"

Kelly laughed briefly, then sobered when she refocused on the mountain of unpacked information on Linda's guest bed. Kelly didn't have time to freewheel about her mother's holiday.

"Mom, did you ever find a box of old letters under my bed when you redecorated my room?" Kelly asked, hoping her mother could think beyond the tequila.

And she did, in typical, always-focused Linda style, "Anything you left I put on the top shelf of the closet. Everything was dusted and cataloged and placed there with care."

Kelly smiled. Even drunk, her mother was in control. No wonder so many family members had compared them over the years.

"Thanks, Mom."

"Do you need me to send you something?"

"No. I'm at the house now. I'll get it while I'm here."

"Wait, *what*? You're in Michigan? *Why*? What's going on?" The drunken celebration was long gone now and Linda wanted answers.

But Kelly was quick on her feet, "I came back with Felix. He had an FBI thing in Detroit so we came by the house."

Linda was silent for a moment, as if analyzing every angle or possible alternative. "You're sure you're okay?"

"I'm fine. Really. I'll call you later, okay?"

"Kelly, you're worrying me—"

"Mom, everything's *fine*. I promise. I love you." Kelly hung up before Linda could protest and turned off her phone to avoid callbacks.

She opened the closet door and sure enough, the top shelf was ridiculously organized—sweaters vacuum-packed in space-saving bags, a dust-free desk fan, and a stack of six labeled shoeboxes.

Kelly grabbed the box marked KELLY'S BEDROOM and set it on top of Fawn's progress reports. And without giving herself a chance to think, she removed its lid.

Inside was a small stack of envelopes rubber-banded together, notebook pages with Kelly's early handwritten ideas for her book, and a handful of newspaper clippings dubbing Fawn the *Motel Murderess*.

But at the bottom of the box, under all the paper, wrapped in a wrinkled hand tissue, was a rusty brass key linked to a red plastic keychain. THE FONTAINE MOTEL was written on it in an old paintbrush-style font, the number 10 circled in its center.

It was crusted with a few drops of blood.

Ford's blood.

Kelly hadn't seen the key since 1996. Overstreet had given it to her after Fawn's case had closed, thinking Kelly would want to keep it. Kelly hadn't, but she hadn't wanted it to go to anyone else either. So it was carefully placed in the old shoebox to be forgotten.

Seeing it again, all the memories of those few short days came back with a vengeance, punching Kelly in the gut, just as fresh and raw now as they had been then.

She rewrapped the key in tissue and delicately placed it back in the shoebox, then pulled out the envelope stack—Fawn's letters to Jill, three of them, chronologically ordered by postmark date.

Kelly opened the first one, dated three weeks after Fawn's arrest.

It was almost two pages, handwritten in soft pencil in Fawn's tiny block-letters. There were no apologies or acknowledgments of her crimes, but rather a scattered rehash of childhood memories and silly anecdotes and randomly scribbled love-hearts. It read like the notes they'd passed each other in Mrs. Brown's AP English course senior year, not like a killer's first letter from prison.

The second letter was a lot shorter, with a chillingly taunting tone.

January 12, 1997

Dear Jill,

Over six months and <u>nothing</u>? Why aren't you writing me? Are you angry or upset with me for some reason? You're not holding a grudge over that mishap at the motel, are you?

Write me.

—Fawn

Kelly actually laughed a little. If prison psychiatrists had read any of Fawn's outgoing letters, no wonder they'd stated she had no remorse for her crimes. That same disregard and blasé attitude carried over to Fawn's final letter to Jill, although with an added level of resentment as it was addressed to JILLIAN 'PRINCESS BITCH' GEORGE.

November 23, 1997

Hello, Your Highness!

You're making a mistake. There's so much more to the story you'll never know if you ignore me. Are you really so selfish you'd rather ignore me than know the truth? You've always been a self-centered bitch.

Guess you'll never know.

—Fawn

Kelly rolled her eyes. She'd researched enough about killers and psychopaths and sociopaths to know a power play when she saw one. There was nothing more to Fawn's story—she *was* the story—but she'd tried luring Jill into her game, a move that had luckily failed.

Kelly stood from the bed and stretched while Fleetwood Mac played softly on the radio. She had no clue what time it was or how long her rocky trip down memory lane had lasted, but she wasn't giving up. She just needed a breather to refocus, and Stevie Nicks always played her heartstrings like a banjo.

Kelly smiled and retook her spot on the bed. She set Fawn's files and the Fontaine snapshots aside and returned to Overstreet's box.

She quickly skipped the folder labeled FONTAINE FORENSICS. There was no way in hell she wanted to see images of Ford's blood in the motel's dirt parking lot or Berger's jawbone on the shag carpet of Room 9.

She opened the folder labeled OLIVER FOSTER instead.

What she noticed first were heavy black-barred redactions striping each page. Single lines, partial paragraphs and complete sections were blackened beyond readability. Kelly had read a lot of redacted files in her work with Overstreet. Survivor and witness statements were often redacted to protect identities, sensitive medical information, or law enforcement's investigative techniques for ongoing cases.

Since Kelly couldn't decipher much about Oliver, she realized his case was protected because of the ongoing Grant Carver manhunt.

Oliver's medical report was less blackened, though, and the long grocery list of injuries he'd sustained in the fall from the fifth-floor balcony had been catastrophic, most of them fatal in themselves let alone collectively. But he'd survived a few hours after the fall, only to succumb to the injuries at the hospital.

He'd suffered immense, excruciating pain, just like Overstreet.

Both men had suffered at the hands of Grant Carver.

There weren't many personal details about Oliver, not that Kelly could understand through the blackouts. But he'd had good grades, was called *fetching* and *witty* by an unknown source, and he'd been in a passionate seven-month relationship with Grant starting in 1994. But there wasn't much else, nothing about *him*—his sense of humor or his favorite movie or the reasons why he and Grant had fallen in love.

Reading his file saddened Kelly. Oliver had taken his own life to escape a killer, yet all the life he'd lived before jumping was summed up in a few unimportant interrupted blurbs. Kelly had fought hard against the same disregard after Ford's death. The press had shorted his wonderful life in similar ways, focusing on his violent death and not his fantastic life.

And even though Oliver's death was part of the story Kelly was trying to uncover, she felt a sudden urge to know what he looked like. She wanted to see his face, but there were no photos in his file other than a few images of bloodstained concrete beside the Marina del Rey apartment's pool, where he'd landed after his fall.

Kelly opened the CARVER CAMERA '95 folder. The first page was a signed statement from a woman named Charlotte "Char" Wolff, declaring she'd found a backpack in her mother's basement that had once belonged to Grant Carver. Inside it she'd found a roll of duct tape later identified as used in four homicides and a disposable camera dated 1995. She'd had it developed and turned in the photographs to the FBI.

The folder in Kelly's hands contained copies of those photos, each page a single color shot with brief handwritten descriptions. The first featured three teenagers in a cafeteria—a young woman and two young men, one of the men kissing the other's cheek. Overstreet's notes read: CHAR, OLIVER & GRANT; HICKORY GROVE HIGH, 1995.

If Overstreet had written the names in the order they appeared in the photo, then the woman on the end was Char, who sat beside Oliver, who was kissing Grant's cheek. Char was beautiful, with long dark hair and porcelain skin and even in the grainy photocopy she had bright violet eyes. Beside her, Oliver was blonde and brightly blue eyed and very handsome, but Kelly quickly lost interest in Oliver and Char.

She couldn't stop staring at the man on the end.

The first image she'd seen of Grant Carver.

He didn't smile at the camera, he *smirked*.

He was broad and beefy, with long shaggy hair and very dark eyes, almost black. He wore a leather jacket and just fucking *oozed* trouble.

The folder contained more photos—Char, Oliver and Grant at an all-night diner, a grainy shot of Eddie Vedder at a Pearl Jam concert, Oliver and Grant sitting on the hood of a Pontiac Firebird. In each picture, the three teens looked wacky and wonderful and lively, like most teenagers, like Kelly's own friends in the instant camera snapshots.

As Kelly flipped through the photographs, they quickly went from wacky to horrific. There were two photos labeled JACK CARVER, featuring a fortysomething man lying on a linoleum floor with duct tape over his goateed mouth and a small forehead gash bleeding into his frightened eyes. After that was a fiftysomething woman—SALLY BARKER—red beehive, duct taped and bloodied, thrown in a ditch; then a thirtysomething man—MALIK KOPSON—olive skinned, duct taped and bloodied, stuffed in a closet with a telephone cord around his neck.

Kelly dropped the pictures and stood up.

Her heart raced and her hands shook.

She opened the window and inhaled chilly air. A slight breeze knocked over Jill, Matt and Ford's snapshot on the bedside table.

There was something animalistic about Grant's killings. Kelly had seen brutality in Mason Strauss's murder—Berger and Fawn killing him with a refrigerator door—but Grant's killings were even scarier. Kelly had thought she'd seen it all in Fawn. She was wrong.

The other photographs were candids between Oliver and Grant—Grant pissing into tumbleweeds; kissing each other on a flannel blanket; Grant brushing his teeth in a seedy motel room; Grant in aviator sunglasses; Oliver flashing a nipple; Grant blowing smoke rings . . .

A seedy motel room.

Kelly flipped back.

Grant stood naked at a sink counter, his ass toward the camera, his face in the mirror's reflection. He stood on red shag carpeting, the walls covered in faux-wood paneling, the bed draped in a pastel paisley-printed bedspread.

It was trashy and dirty and Kelly recognized every goddamn inch.

It was the fucking Fontaine Motel.

She'd been *in* the room before. She and Overstreet had visited the Fontaine together shortly after Ford's murder, to research her book.

And now it was clear: Oliver and Grant had been to the motel too—the first connection linking Grant to Berger and Fawn.

But when? And why?

Grant had been released from police custody and disappeared a year before Kelly's friends had visited the Fontaine, so they couldn't have been there at the same time.

After Oliver died in Marina del Rey and his name was released to the media, Kelly's friend Nate—who'd coincidentally worked at the Fontaine in the nineties—told her he'd once met Oliver at the motel. But Nate hadn't given much detail to the story and he'd certainly never linked Oliver or Grant to the events that had led to him meeting Jill and the others, until now.

Maybe it was a coincidence? Maybe two small groups of friends from neighboring Michigan towns visited the Fontaine at two separate times in the nineties? The motel was in the middle-of-nowhere Oklahoma and wasn't easily accessible by any highway, but . . . *maybe*?

Kelly wasn't a firm believer in coincidences, but until she had any concrete proof or more information, she'd have to take this—and everything else—at face-value. Maybe it really was just a coincidence.

Maybe.

Kelly skipped the VICTIM REPORTS file, assuming they contained autopsy and medical examiners' reports on Grant's victims, and crime scene photos—the last images of innocent people, beaten and battered and bloodied, with intricately-duct-taped bowties on their ankles and wrists, just like Overstreet. Kelly couldn't—*wouldn't*—look.

But she wouldn't skip the CARVER folder, the thickest in the box by far. Her hands shook when she gripped it. She was about to read the history of the man who'd killed her friend, the man Overstreet had investigated for the last ten years of his life, the man Kelly had to catch.

The first page of the file was a yellow sheet with seven names written in Overstreet's lefty scrawl, along with ages and causes of death, like a frightening roll call of the dead of all of Grant Carver's victims:

JACK CARVER, 48; *beaten to death with kitchen counter*
SALLY BARKER, 56; *beaten to death with ketchup bottle*
MALIK KOPSON, 33; *beaten to death with rotary telephone*
PABLO HARVEY, 36; *beaten to death with toilet tank cover*
MELANIE FAZIO, 28; *beaten to death with broken cinderblock*
JULIE BRADLEY, 24; *beaten to death with hammer*

Kelly cried as she added another name to add to the kill list:

FRANK OVERSTREET, 59; *beaten to death with a crowbar/tire iron*

Kelly had avoided crime scene photos to bypass such intricate details, and she'd hoped Grant's file would've started off easy, with shitty high school transcripts or payroll stubs from a dead-end job or childhood dental records, not his goddamn kill list.

Seeing the six strangers' names was terrifying. No photos, just names, like they hadn't been real, just *things* that had met a brutal end. Kelly always wondered what people thought of Ford whenever they'd read his name. Did they just see a murder victim—a *thing*—and not the wonderful man he'd actually been before his death?

The rest of Grant's file was stuffed with similar atrocities:

—medical examiners' in-depth reports and autopsy findings on the victims, from Michigan to Indiana, Missouri to Iowa, and Colorado to Vegas, each exhaustively-detailed on the brutality and unimaginable violence Grant had inflicted on them; Pablo Harvey had been beaten so badly with a toilet tank cover that his jawbone was dust.

—a Pontiac Firebird registered to Grant found in the underground parking garage at the Marina del Rey apartment contained blood, hair, clothing and duct tape fibers that linked him to five of the murders.

—Grant's fabricated statement, describing his bogus self-defense attack against his father that ended in Jack Carver's death, and the subsequent vacating of charges after his release when Jack's death was incorrectly deemed self-defense.

—extensive fingerprint analysis, including a copy of his 1995 fingerprint card from the Hickory Grove Police Department.

—documents on Grant's Marina del Rey apartment and Los Angeles art gallery, both leased with faked, untraceable identification.

—forensic psychologists' reports listing Grant as an opportunistic killer, using everyday items to cause fatal injuries, the spur-of-the-moment weapon selection all part of the thrill. But the theories differed on *why* he killed. His victims were different ages, races, sexes, and none had been sexually assaulted or robbed, but there were plenty of theories—Grant's childhood physical and emotional and possible sexual abuse at the hands of his father (as stated in a few uncorroborated decades-old Child Protective Services case files), or his mother's abandonment, or an undiagnosed mental defect, or a combination of any or all might've made him a killer. But the psychologists all agreed they couldn't know for sure without studying Grant in person.

After Fawn's killings, Overstreet had told Kelly that in all the hundreds of murder cases he'd worked during his long career, he'd rarely received a satisfying answer to *why* any killer killed. More often than not, there were no reasons why. And Overstreet believed it wasn't as important as stopping the killer anyway.

Kelly wasn't sure what she believed, although she'd learned the hard way about not getting answers when Fawn had refused to even *hint* at her reasons why.

But one thing was clear: Grant Carver was a very dangerous man.

Kelly wouldn't allow herself to think about Grant's violent rage and anger, because he'd used it to kill Overstreet. She didn't want to think about her friend's suffering, but she sure as hell wanted to stop Grant from doing it again.

And yet . . . she *still* saw no solid connection to Berger and Fawn.

Why had Overstreet put these three killers in a meticulously-organized file-folder-threesome?

There were plenty of similarities— they'd been under age twenty when they'd killed, they'd slept at the Fontaine Motel, they were from small Michigan towns, they'd been from broken homes.

And Kelly had watched enough episodes of *Hill Street Blues* and *Murder, She Wrote* to know the importance of a smoking gun to close a case, but there wasn't one here, not that she could find.

She read and reread statements and police reports and forensic findings—all written in exhaustive technical and psychoanalytical specifics that meant nothing to her—but found no correlation.

And yet, Overstreet had linked them together.

Why?

Overstreet himself was the only obvious connection in both cases, but he'd been too smart and methodical to lump two unique yet different cases into the same archive box just to save space; there had to be a more specific reason.

Until she could find out, Kelly joined the endless reports' collective consensus on Grant Carver: he was a serial killer, elusive and savage; and he'd proven himself far more sinister in his seven known kills than meek and mousy Fawn had in her three.

And he'd killed Frank Overstreet.

And somehow Kelly just knew Overstreet knew it was possible that Grant might kill him too and that he'd led her to his own killer.

Kelly actually smiled.

It was just like Overstreet to point her in the right direction, to give her the needed tools to get the job done, just like he'd done with Fawn's crimes, just like he'd done for Kelly's life after those crimes.

He'd helped her a lot.

Now she'd help him, by catching Grant Carver.

But Grant was a ghost. Other than a few uninterested attendees, no one but Oliver Foster had seen Grant since the Hickory Grove High School reunion in June. But Oliver was dead.

Except . . .

Actually . . .

Oliver hadn't been the *only* person who'd seen Grant.

Kelly shuffled papers until she found a handwritten contact sheet for Charlotte "Char" Wolff. Char had been Oliver's best friend for over twenty years and she'd exposed the long-awaited proof that Grant was a serial killer. Surely she could fill in the redacted blanks of Oliver's file and his *life*. Plus, she'd attended the high school reunion with Oliver. Presumably, she'd seen and spoken to Grant.

According to Overstreet's notes, Char ran a fashion magazine and lived in Denver. She could potentially get Kelly one step closer to Grant, but would she want to help? Would she want to revisit the past and fill in the blanks? Or had she moved on from Oliver's death and left Grant's destruction behind her? Kelly would certainly understand if she had, but there was only one way to find out.

"How's it going in here?" Felix asked, peeking inside.

Kelly smiled at him and said, "I have to go shopping."

Felix laughed. "Why?"

"I need a better winter jacket, because I'm taking my ass to the Mile High City."

KELLY

Kelly was unfamiliar with Denver, having only visited once during her book tour. Her initial reaction to the city in December wasn't exactly positive. Like Michigan, she rejected the snow and ice and overall wintery nastiness with a deep, passionate hatred.

But her airport taxicab driver was coincidentally from Detroit and kept her distracted from the weather. They talked Motor City concert venues and clubs as he drove her to Char's house, then downtown to the tall building which housed Char's fashion magazine headquarters.

Felix had stayed behind in Detroit to help locally with the investigation of Overstreet's murder, although begrudgingly. He'd wanted to be with Kelly, to help her. But Kelly had insisted. Not only was she unafraid of danger, but everything she'd read on Char Wolff in Overstreet's files suggested she was combative. Kelly didn't want to back her into a corner with herself *and* an FBI agent.

After a brief security check with a very handsome but overly-cologned male officer, Kelly rode the elevator to the twenty-third floor.

When the doors opened, Kelly didn't see any people or hear any sounds, but the floor was full of cubicles and color—fabric swatches and modeling headshots and past issues framed on the walls; neon feather boas and balloons were pinned to leather desk chairs and every cubicle had framed photos of children or pets or Justin Timberlake. It appeared a very happy, inviting, fun place to work. Even with most of the lights turned off—presumably because it was a weekend—the space glowed softly like a sleeping rainbow.

Along the outer wall that faced the street with impressive views of the Denver skyline were several glass-walled offices. Kelly followed the doors' shiny brass nameplates—impressed to see mostly women in powerful positions—and stopped at the corner office at the end: CHAR WOLFF *Editor-in-Chief*.

Through the glass walls Kelly saw a beautiful dark-haired woman about her own age, sitting at a ridiculously-large glass desk in the only subdued space around—no posters, little color, and only a few framed photographs on the wall among white leather furniture and a soft blue area rug. She held a large red marker, circling and striking out images on what appeared to be magazine proofs.

The office and the entire floor were *quiet*—no holiday music or busybody chatter. Kelly liked quiet but this was eerie. But she might've projected its eeriness because of her reasons for showing up unannounced; everything was scarier when delivering bad news to someone . . . and then asking for their help.

Char's door was open, so Kelly tapped her knuckles on it and said, "Only sad old spinsters work on Sundays."

Char looked up from her desk, her pretty violet eyes unamused by the disturbance, and asked, "Can I help you?" Her tone suggested anything *but* an eagerness to help.

Kelly let herself into the room and Char quickly stood from her desk, almost defensively, as if ready to fight. But Kelly smiled and held up her hands, signaling she meant no physical harm.

They were both beautiful—long dark hair, sparkling eyes, flawless skin—and it wasn't lost on either of them.

"Jesus, we look like the Doublemint Twins." Kelly laughed. "You're Charlotte Wolff? Everyone calls you *Char* though, right?"

Char didn't respond, but the attitude on her face said plenty.

"I'm Kelly Spencer." Kelly held out her hand, but Char didn't shake it. It hung awkwardly in the small space between them before Kelly tucked it back inside her warm winter jacket pocket.

Char's face went from uninterested and annoyed to pale white, almost frightened, as if she'd seen a ghost or something even scarier.

When she spoke, her voice was soft and painfully controlled, "*The* Kelly Spencer? Like, the Fontaine Motel Kelly Spencer?"

"I wasn't at the Fontaine Motel, but yes."

Char spot-checked her perfectly-maintained manicure and cleared her throat, as if to jumpstart its volume. "I read your book," she said. "I used to think it was pretty good."

"Used to?"

Char folded her arms against her expensively-dressed chest and held her head high, her eyelids low. "It was good until its author showed up unannounced at my office on a Sunday when everyone else knows not to disturb me when I'm working."

Kelly smiled, partly impressed by Char's refusal to be intimidated, but mostly at the audacity of her attitude. Overstreet's notes had called Char stubborn and outspoken and tenacious. Being in her presence now, in real life, only reaffirmed to Kelly how astute and observant Overstreet had been because he'd perfectly pegged this stubborn bitch.

"I'm sorry to disturb you," Kelly said.

"What do you want?" Char asked.

"I tried you at home. Your neighbor said you were probably here."

"Which neighbor?"

"Uh, to the left of your house. John, I think he said."

Char rolled her eyes quickly, then turned away from Kelly's face.

Kelly's perception and ability to read people had been razor-sharp since she was a kid. Clearly, Char's annoyance was skyrocketing, which in turn flared Kelly's.

"But *why* are you here?" Char asked. "And who the hell said you could talk to my neighbors?"

Kelly wanted to slap the attitude right out of Char's mouth with perfectly-timed precision, like an episode of *Dynasty* or *Knots Landing*, but Kelly smiled instead and refocused. Her love for Overstreet and the need to catch Grant Carver was more powerful than giving Char an open-palm Joan Collins face slap.

So Kelly softened her voice and said, "I need your help."

Char just stared at her, waiting.

"Frank Overstreet is dead," Kelly added.

Char took a deep breath and nodded. She didn't seem surprised, but *confirmed*, and said less aggressively, "I heard. I'm really sorry."

Kelly was pretty sure Char *wasn't*, but didn't say anything.

"The Free Press said it was a mugging?" Char asked.

"*No*," Kelly corrected. "He was murdered."

It hurt to speak those words about her friend. It had hurt with Ford too, but Kelly had spent many years healing and accepting his loss. Would she have to start all over again for Overstreet?

"*Murdered*?" Char echoed. "That's terrible, but what does that have to do with—"

Char's pretty face changed from confusion to recognition. The word *murdered* apparently perplexed her, but now she looked at Kelly with a fierce, deadlocked stare. Kelly could see past memories and future fears all swirl in her violet eyes, just like she'd seen in her own when the truths had been exposed about Fawn and Berger.

Char *knew*.

But Kelly didn't rush her or demand anything.

She just waited, for Char to think and process and breathe.

Finally, Char asked, "You think it was *him*?"

Kelly didn't need clarification; they understood each other.

They were both speaking of the same person, the same *killer*.

"I think it was Grant Carver, yes," Kelly said.

"Please don't say that name in this office," Char instructed.

Kelly nodded with complete understanding. After Ford's death, she hadn't spoken Fawn's name for a long time. She respected Char's need for distance.

"I've read his file," Kelly said. "I know what he's done."

"Oh. Really? You've read his *file*?" Char words were venomous. Suddenly, she was ready to fight. "Tell me, did his *file* describe the way he beat his father to death with his bare hands? Or a hotel manager with a telephone or a waitress with a ketchup bottle or—"

"Or your best friend jumping to his death?"

Char's eyes glistened with incoming tears.

"I know about Oliver," Kelly added. "And their relationship."

"You don't have a goddamn clue." Char wiped her face with tissue dispensed from a sharp-edged silver holder on the edge of her desk.

Kelly stepped back to give Char space. As Char composed herself, Kelly realized how raw Char was. Just six months ago, she'd lost her best friend Oliver to a killer; she was still in the thick of her grief. It had taken Kelly nearly a year to rebuild her life after Ford's death and she now felt like a real asshole for invading Char's healing.

But catching Grant was her priority.

Kelly wouldn't lose sight of that.

Char checked her eyes in a small mirror on the glossy white art-book-stuffed shelves behind her. She dried her tears with tissue and reapplied mascara.

Then Char's voice returned with confidence and a hint of aggression, "I'm told I'm the one who broke the case wide open because of that fucking camera I found in Grant's old backpack. You know, the one with pictures of three of his victims. I almost wish I hadn't."

Kelly wasn't sure why this was Char's starting off point, but she nodded and said, "But that camera also had pictures of you and Grant and Oliver in high school."

"You've seen them?" Char asked.

"Those pictures are the only known photographs of Grant, other than his mugshot from ninety-five."

Char glanced wide-eyed at Kelly, as if this new information only compounded the weight of an already-heavy responsibility.

"All the papers said I was some makeshift hero," Char said. "Like there's some grim honor in exposing someone as a fucking serial killer."

"You don't have to tell me any of this," Kelly said.

"Isn't that why you're here? To learn about Grant?"

"Well, yes, but—"

"Overstreet was a nice person. *Kind*." Char recapped her mascara and took a breath. "He had your picture framed on his office wall. His face came to life when he talked about you."

"He was—" Kelly stopped herself. She wasn't sure how to describe Overstreet to a stranger. Although Char had known him too, there's no way she'd understand the closeness and love Kelly felt for him, but she made sure to point out, "He was a very good friend. *That's* why I'm here, to catch the bastard who killed him."

"Well, Grant was certainly a bastard, but I don't know the first thing about tracking down a serial killer," Char replied. "I'm a fucking fashion magazine editor, not Angelina in *The Bone Collector*."

Kelly understood Char didn't want to relive what had happened to her friend. Revisiting pain in her office—a safe space—couldn't be easy. But Kelly needed answers and she'd had enough of Char's resistance.

"Could you be less of a flippant bitch and *think*?" Kelly asked.

Char tilted her head. "Think about what?"

"I'm sorry Oliver died, but with him gone, you're next in line. You knew Grant, maybe not as well as Oliver, but you knew him. You're the only person alive who knows who the fuck this guy is. So, if there's anything you could tell about him—"

"You don't have to remind me about Oliver," Char snapped. "But thank you for the non-so-delicate condolences."

"Char, he killed a lot of people and he made Oliver jump to his death." Kelly refused to let up, desperate and determined. "I need your help to catch him. Just tell me what he—"

"I don't fucking know! Okay? I don't *know*!" Char's voice shook like thunder. "We didn't like each other. I only put up with him because he was Oliver's deadbeat boyfriend. The three of us went to concerts and record stores and greasy spoons together, but I can't tell you what he was *like* because I didn't give a shit. I mean, he had an asshole father, but you already know that because Grant fucking *killed* him."

Kelly wasn't intimidated or even offended by Char's outburst. It had nothing to do with her, but with Char's insecurities and guilt—irrational or not—that she hadn't been more aware or paid closer attention to the man her friend had dated and she'd spent so much time with. But pushing Char over the edge to this reaction was the first hurdle toward getting answers.

Kelly stood straight, hands in pockets, waiting for Char to cool down and continue.

"Then there's that itty bitty *decade* when we didn't see him," Char snapped, still fiery and *mad*. "He was a ghost. We didn't know where the fuck he was. And surprise, surprise! He's a ghost again. How the hell do you catch a ghost without Dan Aykroyd or Bill Murray, especially when Casper hasn't left any breadcrumbs and has no weaknesses? He's a fucking *killer*, Kelly. So no, I can't tell you what he's *like* or help you find him because I don't have a fucking clue."

"He has one weakness," Kelly reminded.

"Yeah. *Oliver*. You don't think I know that?"

Char stood near the office window, overlooking snowy downtown. She avoided Kelly's face and seemed to lose herself in memories of her best friend. Kelly understood all too well how the memories of lost loved ones could overtake without warning.

"I'm sorry you lost him," Kelly said softly. "It hurts when you lose someone you love."

Kelly could see Char's reflection in the frosty window. She wasn't as lost in thought as Kelly expected, but determined, *focused*.

Char flipped her hair and opened the locked bottom drawer, pulling out a small leather clutch, and said, "Let's go outside."

Kelly shook her head. "My eyelashes grow icicles in that winter wonderland and you want to talk *outside*?"

"You'll be fine, princess," Char groaned. "Zip up that very expensive jacket I'm guessing you bought just to come here, and let's go."

Char threw on a long black fitted wool coat and left her office in long, confident strides.

Kelly matched her step for step.

They didn't speak during the elevator ride to the ground floor.

When the revolving doors swirled them onto the street, a chilly wind gust pierced against their perfectly made-up faces.

"*Fuck!*" Kelly frantically wrapped herself further into her jacket, popping the faux-fur-lined hood over her head and tightly tucking her hands under her arms. "You know you can pack a bag and leave, right? You don't have to live in a place like this on purpose."

Char laughed. "We grew up in *Michigan*."

"Yeah, and I got the hell out of there as soon as I could."

Char pulled out a pack of Camel Lights from her clutch and asked, "You want one?"

"I don't smoke."

"Goes against your puritan sensibilities, huh?"

Kelly had plenty of reasons for not smoking, none of which were anyone's business, and her defenses roared, "I once saw a video of two people I thought were friends almost kill a convenience store cashier to steal a carton of Marlboro Lights, so I'm a little cagey when it comes to cigarettes."

"Oh. Yeah. I remember that from your book," Char said, possibly as an indirect apology for overstepping, although Kelly doubted she'd ever apologized for anything in her life.

"I just want to find him, Char," Kelly said.

"I know," Char said softly with the most compassion she'd shown all morning. "I do too." She lit a cigarette and took a long drag, the smoke and her breath swirling in white clouds around them.

When Kelly sniffed the smoke, she remembered riding in Berger's van and sitting around Jill's swimming pool and watching movies in Ford's basement while her friends had smoked. Other than Berger, none of them had particularly enjoyed it but they'd always been misfits and wannabe-badasses, doing anything they weren't supposed to do.

After a few puffs, Char relaxed and said, "Sorry I've been ripping your head off and shitting down your neck. I get a little wound up when I have to talk about *him*."

"Why did you bring me out to Siberia to tell me that?" Kelly asked.

"I can't talk about this inside, just in case."

"Just in case of what?"

"Jesus! Don't you remember the great crime shows of the seventies and eighties? People's offices were bugged left and right."

"Like Sabrina's hotel room in the *Charlie's Angels* pilot? Yeah, I remember. So what?"

Char puffed and exhaled. "We're not sure if he's listening."

"*Who*?" Kelly couldn't make sense of this nonsense.

Char hugged herself and leaned against the building and ashed, then nodded to a black sedan with tinted-windows parked along the curb on the other side of the street.

"See that car over there?" she asked.

Kelly thought she saw two large men sitting inside it, but it was too cold and gusty and all-around miserable for her to accurately focus, and asked, "What about it?"

"And did you notice the cute guy at the security desk?"

"Good suit, too much cologne? What about him?"

Char checked the empty streets, then whispered, "*FBI.*"

Kelly was fiercely focused now. "What do you mean?"

"They've been following me for months. To the grocery store, to yoga, on *dates*. Everywhere. They even live in the fucking house next door to me. My so-called neighbor John you met earlier? He's FBI too."

Kelly's chest tightened, not just from the bitter air, but for the compassion she felt for a woman who needed protection from a killer.

"They think Grant will come after you?" Kelly asked.

"Yes. We never liked each other and I was always an asshole to him, so he probably wants to kill me." Char cracked an awkward smile. "I guess that joke's only funny if he *doesn't* kill me."

Kelly smiled. She always used sarcasm to deflect severity too.

Maybe she and Char were more than Doublemint Twin lookalikes; maybe they were similar in other ways. They were both sassy and outspoken and independent and beautiful.

Maybe they could be friends.

They'd make a fierce duo.

Or kill each other.

Kelly was losing focus.

The sidewalk was sub-zero and her teeth chattered.

"If he's following you," she said. "Is it safe to be on the street?"

"You mean, just in case he's in a sniper's perch somewhere with me in his crosshairs?" Char shook her head and added, "Grant doesn't use guns. At least on the street I have a chance to run."

Both women looked at each other in disbelief, as if neither could believe the conversation was real. And yet here they were—discussing a killer's M.O. and evacuation plans in the event of an attack. The Doublemint Twins never had to put up with this shit.

"Look, the truth is—" Char smoked and avoided Kelly's face.

"What is it, Char?"

Kelly wasn't pushy, just impatient.

And fucking *cold*.

Finally, Char looked in Kelly's eyes and quietly said, "If you're going to catch Grant, you need to know everything."

"That's why I'm here," Kelly said.

"No, I mean *everything*."

Kelly wasn't sure what that meant and her patience expired.

"Char, I'm freezing my tits off!" Kelly snapped. "If you've got something to say, spit it out!"

"Oliver's alive."

Kelly closed her mouth.

Her teeth stopped chattering.

There were no breath clouds.

She didn't breathe.

She couldn't.

She must've misunderstood.

Oliver's alive.

She hadn't heard that correctly.

She couldn't have.

Oliver wasn't alive.

He'd jumped five stories and splattered onto concrete.

Hadn't he?

News reports and official FBI files had confirmed it.

But . . .

Then again . . .

Kelly remembered Oliver's heavily-redacted file in Overstreet's archive box. It could've been a smokescreen to protect Oliver, to bury the truth of what had—or hadn't—really happened. If he'd been in protective custody or witness protection, Overstreet would've fabricated and redacted the file and left the true outcome of Oliver's jump—that he'd survived—a well-guarded secret.

Kelly couldn't believe she hadn't connected the dots. She'd always been relatively optimistic, but she'd never seen people come back from the dead, except on *Days of Our Lives*, but suddenly it all made sense.

Oliver was alive.

"You're sure?" she asked, just in case she'd misunderstood.

Char lit another smoke, took a ridiculously long drag that would shame the *Alice in Wonderland* caterpillar, and said, "Only a few people know. Me and Overstreet and some FBI higher-ups."

"For witness protection?"

Char nodded, as if she'd suddenly lost her voice or vocally confirming it would betray the tightly-guarded secret.

"Did he actually jump or was that a cover story?" Kelly's questions came in quick-fire succession. She wanted answers *fast*.

"Oh, no, he jumped! And he survived, *barely*." Tears flooded Char's eyes, but she didn't cry, like she wouldn't allow herself to do it, like she'd done it enough already.

Kelly was confused. She'd seen pictures of Grant's posh Marina del Rey apartment building. She didn't know how the hell anyone could've survived a jump from the fifth story.

"*How*?" Kelly asked.

"He's a medical miracle." Tears escaped Char's eyes and rolled down her cheeks, slowly, nearly freezing in the bitter cold. "He broke his shin bones, his left forearm and wrist, and popped his spleen like bubblegum; he had a concussion and plenty of cuts and contusions and all kinds of shit. He looked like an extra in *Fight Club*."

Kelly couldn't blink, the cold air burning her eyes.

"He should've died," Char added. "He *wanted* to die. But he didn't. He's always been . . . *unique*." She smiled, almost proud, and a little awkward, like she too couldn't believe this was real.

"How did he—I don't—" Kelly laughed, stunned. "What the *fuck*?"

Char continued, "He spent two months in the hospital, letting his bones heal and hitting therapy *hard*, all under FBI protection. Overstreet only allowed a few doctors and me to see him. The doctors knew Oliver would survive, but Overstreet made a bogus announcement to the press so Grant would believe he died. After the top secret hospital lockdown, Overstreet moved Oliver to a secret location to finish his recovery. He's got a fake name and a job now and he's living this weird fake life to stay safe while they search for Grant."

"Were you in California when he jumped?"

"No. He jumped the day after our ten year high school reunion—gag me!—and Grant actually fucking showed up for it." She rolled her eyes and smoked. "As I'm sure your in-depth *files* told you, Oliver was over the goddamn moon and he and Grant decided to give it another go, so they flew to California together the day after the reunion."

"And you stayed in Michigan?"

Smoke billowed from Char's mouth like a burning haystack, like she could set fire to the past the faster she smoked.

"Yeah. I found his backpack in my mother's basement the day they left," she said. "I found the camera, had it developed, and the rest is serial-killer-exposing history. As soon as I showed Overstreet the pictures he just seemed to *know* what they were, like they confirmed something for him. And they did. We went over his file on Grant—your bible for this quest, I'm guessing—and pieced the puzzle together of everything Grant has done."

Kelly held her breath and just listened.

"Overstreet and I flew to California the night Oliver jumped. Overstreet took control of everything—locking down the hospital, announcing Oliver's fake death, searching for Grant. He was a fucking *boss*," Char said. "But it wore him down and broke his heart, seeing Oliver suffer and not being able to catch Grant. After he got Oliver into witness protection in September, he handed the case off to someone else and went back to Michigan. He never told you about any of this?"

Kelly shook her head. She was sad knowing Overstreet had struggled with Oliver's case. Overstreet had often gotten personally invested in his cases, like her friends' case that had brought them together, and she wasn't surprised it had happened again; she just wish she'd known and could've helped him.

"He didn't talk to me about his cases involving young people and murder," Kelly said. "He was sensitive to my past."

Char smiled softly. "He was a hell of a guy."

Kelly smiled too.

He sure was.

"I tried to help him find Grant," Char continued, freely spilling her guts now that she was on a roll and heavily nicotined. "But he was concerned for my safety so I stayed at the hospital with Oliver for my own protection too. Then Overstreet sent me back here in August, a couple weeks before moving Oliver into witness protection. That's when I got my bodyguards and life's been on edge ever since."

Kelly assumed Char was violating plenty ethical and federal restrictions by sharing this information, and given Char's earlier reluctance and overall sassiness, Kelly wasn't sure why.

So she asked, "Why are you telling me this? I didn't exactly have to use thumbscrews to get you to talk."

"I want Oliver to have his life back," Char answered with a simplistic shrug. "If I can't catch the motherfucker who took it from him, then I'll help whoever can. I guess that's you, Kojak."

Kelly smiled. Even though she had an overwhelmingly big job on her hands, she was ready.

"And I'm telling you for Overstreet," Char added. "He did everything he could to keep Oliver safe. Oliver's *alive* because of him. The least I can do is repay his kindness. But don't tell anyone I was kind."

They laughed.

"I'm just sorry I can't really tell you anything more."

Kelly thought for a moment, then asked, "What did Grant look like at the reunion? All I have are those shitty photos from ten years ago. I have no idea what he looks like now."

Char made a nervous face, like she was about to say something scandalous, and she did, "He looks . . . *hot*. He was always hot when we were kids—that whole Christian Slater in *Heathers* thing—but he's even hotter now. Is it absolutely disgusting that I just said that?"

Kelly smiled. "No. Ted Bundy was kind of hot too."

"So was Tex Watson. Not an excuse, just confusing to my libido."

They laughed again. Sarcasm and laughter helped ease the conversation's seriousness. Kelly had always considered herself quick-witted, but this tenacious bitch had her beat.

"He's bigger now, like, *bulkier*," Char added. "He's got shorter hair, but still with a little wave to it and he doesn't have that scruffy beard anymore. It's thicker now, well-trimmed and maintained. And he wore an expensive black suit. Armani, I think. He obviously has money."

"That helps a lot," Kelly said.

"But that was six months ago. I've worked enough photo shoots to know his look can change in an afternoon. If he shaved his head or bleached it like a boyband wannabe, he'd look totally different."

Kelly hadn't considered that.

She'd once bleached her long dark hair to match Jill's so they could be the *Sweet Valley High* twins for Halloween freshman year and no one at school had recognized her.

And she'd seen enough crime films where crooks and criminals and abused wives went undetected in disguises as simple as wigs or eyeglasses. Hell, Lois Lane spent decades without noticing Clark Kent was actually Superman because of a pair of fucking *eyeglasses*.

Kelly was suddenly overwhelmed.

Grant could be anywhere.

He could be any*body*.

She was looking for a murderous needle in a haystack.

How was she going to catch someone who could be anyone?

"I'm sorry I just deflated your sails," Char said. "You just have to look harder and catch this asshole. Like I said, I want Oliver to have his life back. I miss him. I mean, we follow a strict payphone protocol once a month, but big fucking deal. I'm a selfish bitch and I want more than that. I know Grant took a lot of lives from a lot of people, but that motherfucker took Oliver's life too. He deserves to have it back."

"You talk to Oliver once a month?" Kelly asked, almost giddy.

"We have a phone date set for the twentieth of every month," Char said. "He calls the same payphone across town. I dress like an old gypsy beggar woman to disguise myself and take a bus and a car and walk to it so no one can follow me. And he calls me. It only rings twice. If I miss it, he doesn't call again for another month. That's the only way the FBI would allow it. My fake next door neighbor trails me every time too, *just in case*. It's very Sydney Bristow in *Alias*, but without the intrigue and bad dance music."

Kelly's eyes widened.

She could potentially speak to Oliver within minutes.

But Char quickly added, "Don't get excited, Alexander Graham Bell. I can't give you his telephone number because I don't have it. He always calls me, for security reasons."

Kelly believed her. Char had already confessed her greatest withheld secret—Oliver lives!—and had no reason to lie now, but Kelly wouldn't lose momentum and asked, "Do you know where he is?"

Char smoked and stared at her manicure and avoided Kelly's face at all costs. Clearly she knew Oliver's location, but she wouldn't spill *all* her guts onto an icy Denver sidewalk.

"Oh, the cat's got your tongue *now*? Char, please." Kelly had never begged for anything in her life, but she was dangerously close now. "There's no one more qualified to catch that motherfucker than Oliver. I need his help to do that."

"Can't you get his location from the FBI?" Char asked. "There's gotta be someone in there who'd sing like a bird."

"Probably," Kelly agreed. Surely Felix could track down someone in charge of such classified information since Overstreet couldn't have hidden Oliver without internal approval and help. "But you telling me will be a lot faster."

Char brushed ash off her lapels and looked into Kelly's eyes again.

"I'll go alone," Kelly said, "No one will know."

Char took a breath and barely whispered, "*Chattanooga*."

"Seriously? Hasn't he suffered enough?" Kelly snickered and forced a straight face when she added, "What time does the Chattanooga Choo Choo board?"

Char smiled . . . and the smile gave way to laughter.

Kelly laughed too.

And their humor returned.

They laughed loud and long and it bounced off the quiet icy downtown windows and streets.

"I'm serious, Kelly," Char said, still smiling but firm. "Look after his ass. He's been through enough."

"Do you want to come with me?" Kelly offered.

"Why, so we can be the next Cagney and Lacey?"

"Oliver might feel safer if you're there. And I get to be Lacey."

"In your dreams," Char teased. "And look, I'll do whatever I can to help you and I really want to see Oliver, but I can't go with you."

"Char, this is important."

"No shit! What I mean is I actually *can't* go with you. I'm not allowed to see him while he's in witness protection. I'm already breaking a lot of fucking rules telling you where he is."

Kelly hadn't considered that either. Char has risked a lot already. If Kelly went to Tennessee, she'd risk exposing Oliver. She didn't want to put anyone in danger, but this was a risk she had to take. Catching Grant—*stopping him*—was too important. Kelly hoped Oliver would agree, but she suddenly felt very selfish and uncertain.

"Will Oliver want to help me?" she asked.

Char cracked a very small smile. "He'll help you."

Kelly reached out her freezing hand and squeezed Char's forearm as an unspoken thank you.

"It's not easy for you to ask for help, is it?" Char asked.

Kelly deadpanned," What do you think?"

She didn't like showing vulnerability to strangers, but Char wasn't really a stranger anymore.

A stubborn and tenacious bitch, yes, but not a stranger.

Char stomped her cigarette into ground and threw all her smoked butts into the trashcan beside the street, then flipped her hair, her unwavering confidence back with a vengeance, and said, "If I tell you where he is, you have to promise me you'll keep him safe."

"I will," Kelly said.

And meant it.

KELLY
9:39 PM MST

The hotel room lights were turned off except for a single bedside lamp, the room quiet except for the softly humming heat vent cranked on high. Kelly was tired and the low lighting and heat helped her relax.

From the bedside phone, Kelly dialed a long series of numbers, following Felix's strict dial-in protocol to create a secure, untraceable connection. She smiled as she dialed, feeling like an extra in a *Mission: Impossible* episode. Felix was worried about her and taking every precaution to keep her safe on the off-chance Grant was more sophisticated than they thought and had somehow began tailing her. She was confident he wasn't, but she appreciated Felix's concern.

"Are you okay?"

When Kelly heard Felix's voice, she relaxed into the plush hotel bedding and said, "I'm okay."

Felix released a low sigh, as if relieved. "Did you find Char?"

"Yes. She was at her office."

"What is she like?"

Kelly laughed. "She's meaner than a junkyard dog and she could probably catch a bullet between her teeth like the Terminator, but she knows her shit. She helped. A lot actually."

"How?"

"Remember when Shelley Long came back to life in *Hello Again*?"

"Kel, You know I don't really speak eighties trivia—"

"Oliver's alive."

Felix paused, as if replaying Kelly's words to make sure he'd understood properly. When he spoke, his voice was confused, "*What*?"

"You didn't know?" Kelly was certain he hadn't or he would've told her, but she wanted to be thorough.

"No. I didn't. When my department took over Grant's case, we were told Oliver died, just like everyone else. There wasn't even a *hint* that anything had been covered up. Where is he, witness protection?"

"Yes."

"Wow. Overstreet was good. He must've buried that deep."

Kelly updated Felix on everything she'd learned—from Oliver's miraculous survival to Grant's current physical description to the painful Colorado winter wind—until she'd reached her next step.

"I know where he is," she said. "I'm going to see him tomorrow."

"Where?" Felix asked.

Kelly couldn't bring herself to reveal Oliver's location, even to trustworthy Felix. Overstreet had kept it a secret for a reason—to keep Oliver safe—and Kelly didn't share secrets that weren't hers to reveal, even though she'd pressured Char to do just that.

But Felix didn't pressure her or demand anything. He knew her too well for that. Instead, he said, "Please be safe. It's dangerous for you to expose him."

"I will and I know."

Kelly's throat hurt suddenly, all the day's truths and Overstreet's beaten face and Oliver's injuries and *everything* slowly rising up.

She was going to cry.

Again.

Her overwhelming self-imposed responsibility to catch Grant was already taking a painful toll and she'd only just begun.

"I thought I was done this with, with *death*," she whispered, her words broken and sharp. Her eyes watered and rolled down her freshly-washed face. "Mason and Berger and . . . *Ford* and . . . *Overstreet*. Isn't that enough? After Fawn went to prison, I thought I was done with killers and murder and all this movie-of-the-week shit."

"Kelly—"

"Now I have to *Veronica Mars* my way through another fucking mystery to catch an even deadlier killer? I have to talk to some poor bastard in witness protection to pump him for any information that might help me catch a Bundy-wannabe?"

"No, you don't," Felix said softly. "Kelly, you don't have to get involved, not this time. Let the FBI handle it—"

"Like they've handled it the last six months? If they'd handled it properly, Overstreet wouldn't be dead and Grant would be in jail!"

Felix didn't respond, as if giving Kelly space to breathe fire and let her fury rage.

"But maybe I should!" she barked. "Maybe I should just give up and save my own ass and stay the hell away from Grant Carver!"

She threw a pillow across the room.

And sat up straight.

And gulped the last of the white wine beside the bed.

And took a long, deep breath.

And wiped her face.

And said, "I just . . . I can't give up. I can't let some maniac *asshole* get away with killing my friend. I can't. I *won't*."

"There you are," Felix said sweetly. "Welcome back."

Kelly cracked a smile.

Goddamn, he was good for her.

Overstreet had been one hell of a matchmaker.

"I'm sorry," she said quietly. "I'm just tired and cranky."

"It's okay."

And it was.

"Will you stay on the phone with me until I fall asleep?" she asked.

They'd had plenty of late-night long-distance phone calls while Felix was on assignment or Kelly was on a speaking tour, but Kelly needed his comforting deep voice now more than ever.

"Of course," he agreed. "Do you want to hear about Steve McQueen's Ferraris or Porsches?"

"What's that movie he's in with Ali MacGraw?"

"*The Getaway*."

Kelly's eyelids were heavy.

She snuggled into the fluffy bedding.

"What's the car he drives after the robbery? Tell me about that."

"Ooh. Good choice. The Ford Galaxie 500 . . ."

Kelly smiled into the pillow.

And slept.

KELLY

The Exposure Gallery was on the beautifully manicured Chatta-nooga riverfront, near the aquarium and art museum. The neighbor-hood was lovely, with more December greenery and sunshine than Kelly expected. She was tired from so much traveling, but her rental car was warm and she found a metered parking spot in front of the gallery.

From the street, Exposure had a glass-windowed storefront, re-flecting warm winter sun. A modest string of white Christmas lights hung around the store's sign and front door.

A bell dinged when she entered.

The vast inside space was empty of customers and smelled like bergamot. Framed photographs in a various sizes hung on the walls, mostly images of the surrounding neighborhood or the nearby Great Smoky Mountains, and a small live Christmas tree decorated with mini-camera ornaments stood near the reception desk.

Seconds after Kelly arrived, a well-dressed man appeared from a door at the rear of the gallery. He was broad and handsome, almost too-handsome, with short sandy-blonde hair, a sharp clean-shaven jaw, and piercing blue eyes, like a Hollywood actor from the early-sixties. Paul Newman, maybe? He certainly didn't look like anyone who'd sur-vived a five-story plummet and relearned how to walk.

He looked happy and healthy and *alive*.

Kelly knew he was Oliver Foster, even though he was nearly thirty and a matured man now. His eyes and smile still had the same youthful innocence she'd seen in the pictures from 1995.

"Welcome to Exposure," he said. "May I help you?"

"Are you Jake Ryan Loeb?" Kelly asked, knowing Oliver had taken his love for Jake Ryan from *Sixteen Candles* and Lisa Loeb's song *Stay* as his inspiration for the undercover name. She'd recognize an eighties or nineties pop culture reference from a mile away.

"I am. May I help you?" Oliver stood tall and confidently with his hands in his pockets, but he wasn't smug. He was approachable and casual, his dress shirt sleeves rolled to his elbows.

Kelly stared at him and smiled, wondering how he'd survived shattering his bones on concrete and could still stand so tall and proud.

She smiled and asked, "Can we talk in private?"

"We can talk here." Oliver playfully gestured to the customer-free surrounding. "We're alone."

Kelly nodded to a security camera in the corner above their heads and asked, "Is that recording audio?"

Oliver's eyelids lowered, as if finally suspecting this pretty, dark-haired woman wasn't looking to decorate her summer cabin in the mountains with fine photography.

"Is something wrong?" he asked.

"My name is Kelly Spencer. Do you know who I am?"

"Should I?"

"My best friend Ford was murdered at the Fontaine Motel a year after you were there with Grant Carver."

Oliver's chest enlarged once and froze, but his face remained focused and unflinching.

"I don't know what you mean," he said.

If Kelly hadn't known he was lying, she probably would've believed him. He had a convincing poker face, no doubt a skill he'd perfected after so much time hiding from a monster.

"I'm sorry about your friend," he calmly added. "But I've never even heard of that motel or—"

"I know who you are, Oliver," Kelly interrupted, using his real name to crack his cover story.

Oliver's face lost confidence and his chest sunk. "Who are you?"

Kelly stepped closer to him and quietly said, "Let's talk in private."

Oliver's Adam's apple bobbed as he swallowed hard. He pointed toward the rear of the gallery and said, "My office."

Kelly followed him into a small room. It was meticulously organized with color-coded files on bookshelves, neatly-stacked film proofs, perfectly-sharpened pencils, and not a speck of dust to be found. Kelly quickly suspected his file had redacted his battle with obsessive compulsive disorder; the office indicated Oliver was desperate to keep control of little physical things since he couldn't control any bigger ones.

There was a running computer on a shiny chrome desk. Kelly stepped around Oliver and sat in the plush leather chair in front of it.

She double-clicked the Yahoo icon and typed in her own name. Hundreds of hits were returned, including pictures of herself and her book, and news stories on countless speeches she'd given to college campuses and high schools about violent crime prevention and recovery.

Oliver watched Kelly fly around the web, studying every picture and story she opened. When his hands started to shake, he tucked them under his arms. Kelly saw a large scar on his left forearm, presumably from the jump.

"I'm legit," she said. "And I need your help."

"You're Overstreet's Kelly?" Oliver whispered. "Are you FBI?"

"No, but he's the reason I'm here."

Oliver shook his head. He was confused and scared and everything all at once, and said, "I don't understand. He's the only one who knows I'm here. Well, him and—"

"Char?"

Oliver took two steps back, clearly frightened and unsure of Kelly's intentions, like she knew too much about him and his past and he knew nothing of her.

"She told me where you are. I saw her in Denver yesterday."

"What's going on?" Oliver asked quietly, as if his words were gunpowder and too much volume might explode everything.

Kelly searched Overstreet's name in Yahoo and clicked on a Detroit Free Press story about his murder.

She pointed to the screen and said, "Overstreet's dead."

Oliver leaned closer to read the headline. DECORATED FED KILLED. He covered his mouth with both hands to muffle a cry. Kelly saw a scar on his right wrist.

"His body was found Friday morning," she said. "His mouth and legs and hands were duct taped and . . . his skull was smashed."

Oliver closed his eyes.

Like Char, he just seemed to *know*.

And he didn't appear surprised.

"It was Grant?" he asked, although it wasn't really a question.

Kelly could sense Oliver carried a lot with him—guilt, shame, pain. She carried all that too, but hers wasn't as fresh as his. Being the one to tell him such horrors and add to the burdens he already carried hurt Kelly. She'd spent a decade helping people heal from their pain, yet here she was causing more.

"Yes," she said. "It was Grant."

Oliver released a soft, wounded cry and braced himself against the desk with both hands.

Kelly stood from the chair and helped him sit down.

She leaned against the desk's edge and held his hand. His skin was soft, the scar on his wrist even smoother.

Oliver didn't cry, but his eyes watered as he stared at the screen, reading and rereading Overstreet's fate in black-and-white.

"I can't— He was— I don't—" Oliver rubbed his face. When he looked at Kelly again, his electric blue eyes dimmed slightly and he whispered, "Overstreet saved my life."

"Mine too," Kelly said with a small smile. "And my friends'. He saved us all."

"Is it because of me? Did I get him killed?"

Even if that was indirectly true—Grant retaliating against Overstreet because of his connection to Oliver—Kelly would never confirm it. She didn't believe it was true anyway since only Grant was responsible for his actions and she'd never allow Oliver—or anyone—think they were to blame.

"No," she said softly. "You didn't get Overstreet killed."

Oliver tilted his head slightly, his eyes once again caring and bright, as if he suspected Kelly withheld much more than she gave, but grateful she was potentially sparing his feelings.

But be still nervously asked, "Am I compromised? Does Grant know where I am?"

Kelly hadn't considered this.

Questions kept appearing like an episode of *Pop-Up Video*.

And she didn't have a goddamn answer to any of them.

But Grant wouldn't have tortured Overstreet for Oliver's location; he believed Oliver was dead. Everyone did. Plus, Kelly knew wholeheartedly Overstreet would've taken Oliver's location to the grave anyway. He would've died before giving in to a serial killer's demands.

"Grant thinks you're dead," Kelly assured. "You're not in danger."

"No, but I am stuck in this shithole until Grant gets caught," Oliver said. "It's like hiding under a goddamn rock. At least Deloris Van Cartier got to teach nuns how to sing when she was hiding out."

Kelly laughed.

She liked this guy, a lot.

She liked anyone who kept their humor despite shitty backstories.

Plus, she loved a good pop culture quip.

"At least they deliver pizza to this sewer, Donatello," she offered.

Oliver smiled sincerely, like he liked her too.

"Your friend was killed at the Fontaine Motel?" he asked, as if he needed confirmation that they shared more than a mutual respect for Frank Overstreet, that Kelly too had a violent, painful past that qualified her to understand him.

Kelly nodded. "His name was Ford. He was shot in the back with a twelve-gauge shotgun by someone I thought was my friend. Then she killed her own boyfriend, and shot someone you met once."

"Who?"

"Nate James. He worked the front desk at the motel."

Fresh tears flooded Oliver's eyes and poured down his smooth cheeks. "She shot Nate? Did he . . . *die*?"

"No." Kelly smiled. "He's married to my best friend Jill."

Oliver sighed and laughed awkwardly. "This is so fucking weird."

Kelly laughed too. It *was* fucking weird—two small town strangers connected by a shithole motel and violence and a mutual friend. The world was small . . . and fucking weird.

"Oliver, I understand betrayal and I understand loss. I've lived it." Kelly stared into his ridiculously-beautiful blue eyes. "And I'm so sorry to ask you this, but I need your help."

Oliver stared at her, his face soft and interested, not immediately dismissive, and his interest gave Kelly the courage to keep going.

"I loved Overstreet very much," she said. "Grant has gotten away with a lot, as you know. But I can't let him get away with this too. And you knew him better than anyone else."

Oliver's interest quickly turned defensive, "I'm sorry, Kelly. You obviously came here for answers or clues or *whatever*, but the truth is I don't *want* to remember, for reasons I don't have to explain to you."

Kelly respected Oliver's need to self-protect. He'd been through a lot and discussing it was painful. She'd read the files and she knew Oliver's complicated, painful history—she had one of her own—but she wouldn't bombard him with any of that now. He didn't need to know she knew the ins and outs of his story. All he needed to know was she was there to help Overstreet . . . and him.

"You loved Grant, in ways you'll probably never recover," Kelly said. "But I need you to tell me about him so I can catch him. Please."

Oliver nodded, as if he understood all the unspoken parts. "Six months ago, I saw him for the first time in ten years. I can't tell you a lot of what happened after that because I don't remember much, but if you want to talk about our first date at Dino's Drive-In in 1994 or when he took his car out of storage and abandoned me in 1995, I can tell you *everything* because I remember all that like it was fucking yesterday."

Kelly smiled.

They shared this reaction too—remembering the past with complete clarity while more-recent painful events were harder to recall. She could remember every detail of rollerskating to Culture Club's greatest hits at Roller Haven in the eighties with her friends, down to the neon-pink laces in their skates, but she couldn't recall the color of Overstreet's sweater on Thanksgiving Day a week ago; she was suppressing certain moments to protect herself, just like Oliver.

But something else stood out: Oliver had absentmindedly mentioned a detail Kelly hadn't read in any of the reports.

"He kept his car in storage?" she asked. "The Firebird?"

"He called it Kitty." Oliver rolled his eyes. "His *Knight Rider* car."

"The same Firebird parked at his Marina del Rey apartment?"

Oliver twitched like he'd been stung, like he couldn't believe Kelly knew such specifics. "I never saw it parked there, but he said it was."

"It was," Kelly confirmed, choosing to withhold what had been found inside it. "You said it was kept in storage though, in ninety-five?"

"He stored it before turning himself in to police. When he got out, he took the car and left. I didn't see him again for ten years."

Kelly's grandmother had taught her to be inquisitive. 'You'll never get anything if you don't ask any goddamn questions,' she'd always said. Kelly was close now, on the brink of the next step, and she just had to ask questions.

"Where did he store the car?" she asked, "In Michigan?"

"Probably. That's where he was jailed," Oliver asked. "I don't know where though. His house didn't have a garage."

"He definitely said it was in storage, like in a storage *unit*?"

Oliver held up his large hands in surrender. "All I know is after he got out of jail, he disappeared. I went to his house and all of his shit was gone—records, paints, clothes, and no car."

Kelly had nearly memorized Overstreet's extensively-detailed files in just a few days, and could reference them like the eidetic movie nerds she loved—*Rain Man* had nothing on her now—and there'd been no mention of Grant Carver ever renting a storage unit.

Grant was released from jail in 1995 when the death of his father was ruled justifiable self-defense, but he hadn't been suspected of being a serial killer yet, as all of his known victims came after his father's murder. So no one, not even Overstreet, would have investigated or kept tabs on his 1983 Firebird.

Now, Kelly suspected it was very important.

She sat at Oliver's computer and opened a new Yahoo tab.

"Isaac has two storage places, one across from Steven's Furniture, one next to ideal Pharmacy," she said. "Does Hickory Grove have any?"

Oliver leaned on the desk, watching her type. "Only one, I think. Next to Penis."

Kelly laughed.

She'd forgotten.

Another memory out of nowhere.

Venus Coney Island, but *Penis* to the crass locals. Berger and Jill had loved the greasy spoon because it had had a secluded smoking section that hadn't asked questions when they were sixteen and heavy smokers. The two of them, along with Kelly, Matt and Ford had clocked many hours there, laughing and eating. Kelly wondered if she'd ever been there the same time as Oliver and Grant. Had she ever passed them without knowing their lives would one day intersect?

"Fuck! I forgot about that place!" She refocused and searched for the known storage units. One had been redeveloped into a shopping center in 2003, the others—one in each town—were still open.

Kelly flipped open her Razr and dialed the first number.

"What're you doing?" Oliver asked. "They won't just give you information about renters."

"These are small towns in Michigan. Yes, they will."

Kelly had always rejected the close-knit, down-home feel to small towns, especially the one she'd grown up in and where her friends had committed their first murder, but now she hoped that trusting community would deliver what she needed.

Oliver appeared less convinced, smiling skeptically. "Kelly—"

"Shut up!" she playfully snapped. "It's ringing."

"All Access Storage! This is Art!"

Kelly held the phone away from her ear. The man's voice was gruff and gravelly and very, very loud, like her cantankerous grandfather after he'd spent too many years on the shooting range without ear protection, cranky because he'd lost his hearing, but unable to admit it was self-inflicted.

"Uh . . . hello. My name is Kelly—"

"Gotta speak up, deary! My ears is shot to hell! Can't hear a damn thing since 'Nam!"

Kelly cleared her throat and spoke louder, "I think my friend might have rented a unit from you!"

"You rented a unit?! Yeah?! *So*?!"

"No, my FRIEND!"

"A friend, huh?! He lose his key?!" Art coughed and hacked and spit out something. "Christ! No one holds onto keys no more!"

Kelly felt trapped in a *Saturday Night Live* skit, imagining a crinkled old man surrounded in hazy cigar smoke, wearing overalls and mishearing *everything*, including the ticks of his own pacemaker.

"What's the name, deary?!" Art shouted.

"Grant Carver."

"What?!"

"Grant! Carver!"

"Gillespie?"

Kelly laughed. "No! *Grant*—"

"Yeah. Yeah, we had a Gillespie rent a unit here many moons ago. Looked like one of them beatniks—scruffy beard, long hair, leather jacket, rotten attitude. I only remember 'cuz he had a fruit fly's name and always smoked them damn cigarettes and drove a loud car like he owned the goddamn place. His kind just didn't belong in this town. This is a nice, quiet pace, ain't it, deary?"

"Yes, sir! Very nice!"

Kelly realized she'd stumbled onto something inadvertently. Could it really be this easy? One phone call—her first—to a small Michigan town yielded a positive lead on Grant?

Inadvertent or not, she'd take it.

She didn't like taking advantage of possibly-confused elders, but if Art had helpful information, she'd freely accept it. And his description of the *beatnik* matched nineties Grant to a perfect leather-jacketed T.

But . . . *Gillespie*?

"Here it is! Armstrong! That's it!" Art shouted. "Got it written right here on the rental card! Gillespie Armstrong! Rented unit sixteen in ninety-five!"

Kelly wrote down the name, circled it and showed Oliver. He smirked and shrugged, clearly not recognizing it.

"Only seen him a couple times since!" Art added. "But the rent's never late!"

"When was the last time you saw him?"

"What?!"

"When did you last see him?!"

"Oh, Christ! Dunno! Not since October!"

Kelly's eyes widened. "October? Of this year?"

"No! October of *this* year!"

"If I come there, can I get into the unit?"

"What?!"

"Can I see the unit?!"

"Won't just open it for anyone, deary! If ya want in, better bring the fruit fly with ya!"

Kelly looked at Oliver. He'd make a good Gillespie stand-in.

"He cut his hair!" she said into the phone. "And shaved his face!"

"I'll be goddamned!" Art chuckled. "There's hope after all! It'll cost ya six dollars to replace the lock! Was five dollars last year but them damn things are expensive!"

"That will be fine."

"What?!"

"That will be FINE! Thank you!"

"I'm here every day 'tween ten and four! Don't be early or late!"

"Yes, sir."

"What's ya name?! I'll write it down so I'll remember yer comin'!"

"Kelly Spencer."

"What?!"

"Kelly! Spencer!"

"*Julie*?! *Hector*?! I'll write that down! Julie Hector for the fruit fly's unit!" Art chuckled and coughed.

Kelly had always envisioned naming her alter-ego something fabulously drag queeny or James-Bond-villainy, like Ritzy Partatown or Cinderella Peepers, not Julie Hector. But she'd struck gold with Art's loose lips, so she'd happily impersonate anyone. Maybe Julie wore too much mascara and a sneer.

"All right!" Art shouted. "I'll see ya when I see ya!"

He hung up and Kelly laughed.

Oliver shook his fingers in his ears and asked with a wide grin, "What the hell was that?"

"Hard work," Kelly answered.

"Who the hell is Gillespie Armstrong?"

"A unit was rented in ninety-five by a beatnik with a bad attitude."

"Sounds like Grant."

"The rent's never been late *and* Grant was there in October."

"Of *this* year? Like, two months ago?" Oliver's voice squeaked.

Kelly wasn't sure if the squeak was excitement of catching Grant, or fear of nearing a serial killer. Only time and building a relationship with Oliver would answer that and she was willing to put in the time.

"Why the hell does he still have a storage unit in Michigan?" Oliver asked with a dismissive laugh. "And under that lame alias."

"What do you mean?" Kelly asked.

"Gillespie Armstrong?" Oliver paused, as if waiting for her to catch on. When she didn't, he said, "*Dizzy* Gillespie and *Louis* Armstrong?"

Kelly still didn't understand.

Oliver rolled his eyes. "I get it you're probably a New Kids on the Block kind of girl, but *come on*," he said, exasperated. "You've got to know a few jazz legends too."

Kelly laughed, impressed by the sudden appearance of a razor-sharp wit she didn't know he had, although it made sense since his best friend Char had the sharpest she'd ever seen.

"First of all," Kelly said with a wide grin and a pointed index finger. "I don't like the condescending tone to your voice regarding my precious New Kids. Jordan Knight was dead sexy in 1989, okay? Second of all, do I look *new* to you? Of course I know jazz greats. My grandmother played nothing but Ella Fitzgerald and Billie Holiday records when I was a kid. What's your point?"

"Grant is obsessed with jazz."

"I thought dickheads with Firebirds listened to Whitesnake or Mötley Crüe."

"He likes all music, but he *loves* jazz. He constantly played mixtapes in the car when we were together. Chet Baker, Miles Davis—"

Suddenly it clicked.

Dizzy Gillespie + Louis Armstrong = Gillespie Armstrong.

A jazz-themed alias.

How the hell had Kelly missed it?

"The Marina del Rey apartment was rented under the name Grant Baker," she recalled. "As in *Chet*?"

"Well done." Oliver nodded approvingly and joked, "Maybe us Girl Scouts will get our detective patches after all."

Kelly laughed.

Oliver was handsome and smart *and* funny.

And he deserved his life back.

Kelly spun the chair toward him to face him and said, "Come to Michigan with me." It wasn't demanding or begging, but a smidge of excitement. "Let's check the storage unit together."

"Uh, *pass*," Oliver said.

"You can be the freshly-groomed beatnik to get us in."

"Still no."

"Oliver, we've only been together a few minutes and we've already uncovered something. We have to see it through."

"So what, we're a team now? The Dynamic Duo?"

He chuckled, but Kelly could sense he wasn't convinced. Either fear or uncertainty or both were holding him back and she respected that. He'd been tucked away in a makeshift life in Tennessee and leaving its hidden safety had to scare him.

But there was a momentum between them, the first hopeful sign since Overstreet's death, and Kelly wanted to keep it going.

"We could catch an early flight and be in the unit by lunchtime," she said, trying hard to keep her tone suggestive, not pushy.

Oliver shook his head.

"C'mon," she said, dangerously close to pleading now. "You can call me Tommy Lee Jones and we'll catch this fugitive together."

Still no.

Kelly needed to back off. She'd disrupted this poor man's fake life.

She was nervous to continue alone, but she couldn't ask Oliver to relive his painful past or force him to be an amateur Hardy Boy with her. She already felt like an asshole for demanding so much from Char back in Denver; she wouldn't do it to Oliver too. He'd helped her find the storage unit lead. That was enough.

Kelly stood from the desk chair and gently squeezed his arm again. "I'm sorry I was a pushy bitch. Thank you for your help. I might come see you again if I have more questions."

"I'm sorry," Oliver said. "It's just—"

"You don't owe me an explanation. I'm sorry I sprang all this on you. Overstreet used to call me tenacious and sometimes I get a little overzealous. I just—" Kelly took a breath to organize her thoughts and chase away fresh tears. "There were times after Ford was killed when I'd forget he was dead. I'd wake up in the morning and feel pretty good, like any carefree, clueless eighteen-year-old. Then I'd remember. Something would make me think of him or wonder where he was and I'd feel it all over again—that awful, painful hurt that he was dead, that he'd been murdered. It went on for a long time, until I started waking up and didn't have to remember anymore. I just *knew*. I almost lost myself to that grief and now that Overstreet's dead, I'm afraid I'll get lost in it again if I don't catch Grant, if I don't know I did everything I could." She smiled and wiped her face. "Thank you for your help."

She left the office . . . but only made only a few steps into the gallery when Oliver called her.

"I won't fly," he said.

Kelly turned back toward the office door. Oliver stood beside it, his arms folded tightly against his chest.

"I won't fly," he repeated. "Too many cameras at airports."

Kelly held back a grin. "No one's looking for you. The world thinks you're dead. And I doubt Grant is sophisticated enough to tap into airport security cams."

Her stifled grin broke free. She'd meant it flippantly, but the truth was Grant had been an active serial killer for at least a decade without capture. No one knew how far his net reached. Kelly didn't believe he had a network of airport security cam hackers, but paranoia made even the most logical Hardy Boy doubt herself.

"We could drive," Oliver suggested. "It's easy to stay hidden on backroads and no-name diners, especially in this part of the country. Detroit's only, like, ten hours from here. We could be there when deaf-as-a-post Art opens the rental place in the morning."

Kelly deadpanned. She appreciated Oliver's offer to extend their amateur sleuthing, but she'd never enjoyed driving, not since living in

California, and a *long* drive this time of year, heading north into the snowy Michigan tundra didn't exactly get her motor running.

Plus, historically, neither she nor Oliver had positive experiences with road trips.

"I passed the last time I was offered a road trip and my friends didn't exactly get their kicks on Route 66," she said. "And from what I know about you, your road trip with Grant wasn't exactly the Woodward Avenue Dream Cruise."

"I didn't say we were taking the Highway to Hell," Oliver quipped. "There will be no mixtapes or murder or the fucking Fontaine Motel this time around."

Kelly laughed, but quickly asked, "Can't we just fly? Please? We can wear those gag glasses with fake mustaches and just *blend*."

Oliver shook his head.

Kelly wouldn't press him any further. She could sense his humor and lightheartedness was forced; he was actually terrified of reliving any of this. And she didn't fault him for that. They hadn't even gotten into the deep nitty-gritty of Grant's crimes, much of which Kelly suspected Oliver didn't know. If Oliver was heartbroken and scared now, with news of Overstreet's killing and some storage unit info, how would he cope with the thick, lengthy files Kelly had in the car, detailing every known gruesome act Grant had committed?

She dreaded that impending conversation, but he'd offered to accompany her to Michigan. So if she had to blast the rented BMW's heater for six or seven hundred miles to keep him committed and on board, she would.

The rest could come later.

"All right," she agreed. "But if this turns into *Smokey and the Bandit*, you have to be Sally Field. *I* get to be Bandit."

Oliver smiled. "Deal."

OLIVER
7:46 PM EST

The first two hours of the drive was peppered with pleasantries. Kelly shared her dating history with Felix—whom she assured was *not* a 1920's cartoon cat or a big-eyed wall clock—and celebrity sightings near her Malibu beach house; Oliver talked photography and weekend jaunts to Nashville for the used record stores; and they both reminisced about their small town Michigan childhoods and time spent in the same locations at separate times, like eating ice cream cones at Uncle Ray's and tailgating in the Farmer Jack parking lot.

Oliver sat in the passenger seat while Kelly drove. There had been no discussion or coin toss. Kelly had just taken the wheel and *drove*. Clearly, she liked being in control. Oliver had spent his life with Char—the most controlling woman on the planet—so he wasn't surprised or threatened by a can-do take-charge attitude. Besides, after such a difficult year, he appreciated being the sidekick instead of the star.

There were plenty of proverbial elephants stuffing the small space between them, but they weren't overwhelming, as if Oliver and Kelly were starting slow, getting to know each other first before sharing painful memories and broken histories and focusing on the real reason they were speeding toward snowy Detroit in a rented BMW.

The headlights were bright on the dark road; the radio played seventies jams with the volume low; the dashboard lights were white and green and blue, illuminating Kelly's pretty face as she drove; and the unpressed hazard button glowed neon red.

That color always reminded Oliver of Grant's Firebird.

During late-1994 and early-1995, they'd driven around for hours in the dark, the neon red dashboard lights casting sinister shadows across Grant's handsome face and sparkling in his almost-black eyes. Sometimes Grant wore aviator sunglasses and the lights reflected as contorted steaks in the lenses.

When Oliver had woken up alone at the Fontaine Motel in 1995, various neon colors from the street sign had swirled in the room's darkness . . . and he'd never slept in the dark again. He wasn't afraid of the it, but of waking up alone and lost again. If he kept the lights on, maybe he'd keep the darkness away.

Still, Oliver couldn't believe he'd agreed to this.

What the hell was he doing?

He'd put on a good front back at the gallery, faking strength and a blasé attitude toward his history with Grant, but the truth was much darker and more painful: he was terrified of this road trip, of what he and Kelly might find in a decade-old storage rental, of Grant himself.

But Oliver couldn't express those fears to Kelly. He barely knew her. Regardless of sharing similar experiences or the kindness in her eyes, Oliver wouldn't allow himself to be vulnerable, not again. He'd fought too hard to live, to protect himself, and he wouldn't give in now.

He just hoped his strong exterior wouldn't crack.

Kelly exited the highway long after Knoxville and pulled into an all-night diner—JERSEY'S: THE GREASIEST OF SPOONS!—and parked the car.

"You eat this kind of food?" he teased. He didn't know beautiful, fit Malibu brunettes ate anything but lettuce and ice. The women on *Baywatch* never ate this shit.

Kelly cocked her head. "Watch your judgments, Judy. We've only got one life. I want a happy one with French fries. Plus, I gotta pee."

Oliver laughed.

Kelly grabbed her large leather bag and they walked toward the front entrance, chilly wind gusting through their hair. The air smelled like rain. In the distance, Oliver saw lightning bolts dance across the sky. A storm was coming.

When Kelly opened the door, a delicious waft of greasy food and loudly-chatting customers and rusted Coca-Cola signs welcomed them.

Kelly playfully glared at Oliver, warning him to abandon his judgments, and she dropped her bag at a table near the front windows.

Oliver couldn't stop smiling. This wacky, wonderful woman reminded him so much of Char. But he couldn't stop watching the lightning periodically illuminate the Tennessee sky. There was more than rain and grease in the air.

"Get me some fries and coffee and a slice of apple pie," Kelly said. "And get whatever you want for yourself. My wallet's in my bag."

She left Oliver at the table and went to the restroom.

Oliver, still smiling, opened Kelly's bag. He hadn't withdrawn any cash before leaving Chattanooga, and hoped Kelly had small bills for their quick dinner.

But his smile immediately disappeared.

Inside the bag was a large, thick stack of file folders, the covers and tabs heavily stamped and handwritten with names and numbers and notes that meant nothing to him.

All except one: GRANT THEODORE CARVER

Oliver's heart skipped two beats.

That name was the reason Kelly was here, and Oliver had spent a lot of time healing because of it, but seeing it printed on a white label by an old typewriter still rattled his healed bones.

When Kelly returned to the table, Oliver hadn't moved.

He couldn't take his eyes off the files . . . or Grant's name.

The incoming storm was already here.

Kelly sat in the chair in front of him, but didn't speak.

"What're these?" Oliver asked, his voice just a whisper. He finally looked at her, her pretty face soft and concerned.

Kelly squeezed his badly-scarred forearm. "Don't open those. I'll be right back." She grabbed her wallet and went to the order counter.

While she was gone again, Oliver returned his gaze to the haunting typewritten name.

GRANT THEODORE CARVER

Oliver had doodled that named in his spiral-bound notebooks in high school, like a lovesick teenybopper. And in those days, he was—a teenager *and* lovesick for Grant Carver.

That sickness had overflowed into his adulthood and soaked every inch of it. He hadn't been able to take photographs that weren't influenced by Grant; he hadn't allowed himself to love Giancarlo the way he'd loved Grant; and he hadn't been able to love himself without wondering if Grant would've approve of his decisions.

And when Grant had finally returned six months ago—ten *years* since the last time since anyone had seen him—Oliver's lovesickness had only worsened. He'd been unable to see beyond a powerful, instinctual need to be with Grant that everything else became cloudy, including his judgment and the truth that Grant was a killer.

Kelly returned with a brown plastic tray, carrying two orders of fries, coffees and steaming apple pies slices.

Oliver's appetite vanished. He couldn't even think about food. He couldn't think beyond the information in Kelly's bag . . . and the many years and tears he'd given Grant.

"How much did Overstreet tell you about him?" Kelly asked, shaking a salt packet onto her fries. "About what Grant's done?"

Oliver shrugged.

He wasn't sure.

He couldn't remember specifics.

But the most important bullet points were bold and hard to forget—Grant was a serial killer, Oliver had spent a third of his life loving him, and he'd tried to escape him by killing himself.

"I know you want to read those files," Kelly said, slowly sipping her coffee, as if deliberately taking her time, all the while her tone compassionate, not pitying. "I also know what you did to yourself because of him."

Oliver looked at her again, her face still caring and kind. He felt safe with her, yet terrified of what they were about to discuss. Everything he'd hoped to avoid in the rental car was now bubbling to the surface, ready to blow.

"It's not the treasure map to One-Eyed Willie's rich stuff in there," Kelly added. "Those files—the ins and outs of a duck's asshole about Grant's crimes—will *hurt*. I just want you to be ready."

The leather bag sat on the chair beside Oliver and he was certain the chair was sinking, growing heavier by the second, as if its contents compounded its weight and made it too heavy for the chair to hold.

And Oliver didn't know *how* Kelly knew, but she knew.

He *wasn't* ready.

So he started slowly and asked, "Are any of those files about me?"

Kelly nodded. "Your file is mostly redacted. I didn't know why until I found out about the witness protection."

For some reason that hurt Oliver, like he hadn't been important enough in the story of his own life—or Grant's—to gain full disclosure.

He took the second coffee cup off the tray and swallowed a large gulp. It was too hot, burning his tongue and throat, but he didn't react or even care. He was numb and scared and he couldn't stop staring at the fucking files beside him.

Kelly set the bag on the floor, out of his sight.

He nibbled on a French fry, trying to find direction, a starting off point to get answers to the many questions burning him worse than the boiling coffee.

Kelly was the first to rip off the Band-Aid, "You tried to end your life." She spoke kindly, but matter-of-factly, without adding any *That-took-guts* or *You-poor-thing* sentiments, as if she'd been well-trained in speaking to attempted-suicide survivors.

Oliver appreciated her candor. She was direct and fearless enough to confront the ugly parts of his past instead of avoiding them.

He liked this woman; he felt understood and respected without judgment; and brave enough to say, "Yes, I did. *Twice*."

Kelly sipped coffee, as if waiting for more, giving Oliver plenty of space to take his time and move at his own pace.

"But it wasn't like the movies," he quietly added. "Where the hero falls off a building and keeps fighting with a broken leg or a bullet in his shoulder. I didn't have any fight left in me."

"You wanted to die?"

Oliver sucked in a breath and whispered, "*Yes*."

He'd only said that aloud a few times to therapists. He wasn't ashamed of it, but saying it out loud to Kelly Spencer in a brightly-lit greasy spoon made it more real. And yet *okay*.

"I lied about it for a while," he said. "I tried convincing Char and the doctors and *myself* that I was just trying to save myself from Grant since I'd just learned he was a killer. But it wasn't true. I wanted to die. I wanted to get away from him, for good. So I jumped."

"Do you wish you were dead now?"

Oliver smiled. "*No*."

He'd been through intensive physical and emotional therapy, which had helped him walk again and healed his broken parts, but the old pains could rise to the surface quickly, fresh and raw and real.

"I'm happy I survived," he said.

"*But*?" Kelly asked.

Goddamn, she was perceptive.

She didn't miss a fucking thing.

"I feel so foolish for letting him into my life," he confessed. "For giving up everything for him, almost *literally*, and for sleeping with him and loving him and not seeing who he really was."

Kelly drank coffee and ate pie, as if allowing the dust of Oliver's self-depreciation to settle before saying, "You're not a fool, Oliver. He fell into your blind spot. We have epically huge blind spots when we're teenagers. He was in yours."

Oliver smirked. "Kelly, parents have blind spots when their kids shoplift CDs at Blockbuster Music. I was blind to *murder*."

"So your blind spot was . . . *murkier* than most."

They managed a little laugh and it broke some tension.

"And although I'm no love expert," Kelly added. "I'm *pretty sure* the guy who's made you cry more tears than Claire Danes in *My So-Called Life* isn't your soulmate."

Oliver smiled.

She wasn't wrong.

He'd shed a lot of tears over a lot of years for Grant Carver.

And he was doing it again now.

He wiped his face with scratchy napkins from a Pepsi dispenser.

Thunder rumbled.

Customers came and went.

The grill sizzled and spit with each new burger.

Life continued around them.

It had a really annoying way of doing that.

"I have a lot of questions about him," he told Kelly. "Like, why didn't he kill me too? Why did he come back for me after ten years and bring me into his shiny world of expensive art and great sex and a fishbowl apartment at the beach if he was a killer? How could he love me and want to commit to me *and* be a killer?"

Kelly's eyes widened, like he'd struck an unknown nerve she didn't know how to nurse, and said, "I don't have answers to any of that. I can't even remember the security questions to my eBay account, so I have no idea how to read a murderer's mind."

Oliver smiled. The way Kelly delivered a joke was so much like Char. Punchy and self-depreciating, yet confident and defusing.

"But I will say this," Kelly added. "Overstreet once explained that in so many of the cases he'd seen with criminals over the years—we're talking psychos out of the old Hitchcock movies—that the reasons why rarely make any sense and that sometimes there are no reasons why."

Oliver respected Overstreet, but he didn't like this explanation.

"And even if we find him, you might never get the answers you want. I didn't," Kelly said. "Fawn never told anyone why she killed anyone. Overstreet had his theories of a god complex or attention-hungry or whatever, but she never confirmed or denied any of his theories. So, I know the *hows* and *wheres* and *whens* of what she did, but not the *whys*. I never will. You might never know either."

Before Grant, Oliver had lived a regulated life of answers—math questions answered by Mr. Russell in Algebra I, a nonnegotiable weekday curfew enforced by Mom and Dad, a firm *no* from Char on trying a nicotine patch.

After Grant, Oliver had never been satisfied with much of anything—his photography was never good enough even though it was hugely successful, his relationships weren't with Grant even though he'd been passionately loved by Giancarlo, and his self worth was worthless even though he'd survived death twice.

Grant had taken away Oliver's regulation and his confidence and his will. And hearing Kelly bluntly deliver a harsh truth that he and the rest of Grant's victims might never know the answer to *why* was just another overwhelming blow.

"That sounds . . . fucking awful," he said with a defeated laugh.

"It is," Kelly agreed. "But you learn to live with it. You can learn to live with anything if you have no choice. I don't have to explain the alternative, because you know better than anyone what happens if you *can't* live with it."

Oliver pushed the now-cold fries around the plate. Slicing a few of them through a pool of ketchup reminded him of the small speckles of ketchup he'd once cleaned off Grant's arm in the Firebird.

But they hadn't been ketchup specks.

They'd been droplets of blood.

Grant had murdered a waitress minutes before.

Sassy and beehived Sally had run tables and the skillet at Barney's Burger Booth in the middle of the night. She'd gifted Oliver and Grant fresh strawberry pie slices with sky-high dollops of whipped cream, and she'd told Grant he'd had enough charm to choke a snake.

She'd been kind to them . . . and Grant had bludgeoned her to death with a ketchup bottle and dumped her body behind the diner.

And Oliver hadn't had a clue. Instead, he'd cleaned not-ketchup off Grant's arm and drove the Firebird on a strawberry pie sugar rush all the way to the Fontaine Motel, where everything had changed.

Thunder rumbled outside.

Oliver glanced out to the dark horizon.

Lightning flashed.

Seconds later, rain poured.

The storm was here.

The diner's outdoor sign—illuminated in pink and red neon strips—blurred and swirled in the rain. In 1995, Oliver had awoken in Room 10 of the Fontaine Motel, alone, with similar neon strips filtering into the darkness, the street sign beaming through the window.

Grant had left Oliver there, *alone*.

It had rained then too—heavy, pelting, brutal rain.

Oliver's tears had blurred and swirled with the lights then, and it happened again now as he watched the rain smack and pound against the diner windows.

"Grant left me in the middle of the night at the Fontaine," Oliver said quietly. "It was dark and raining and he . . . *left*. I've never slept in the dark since. Not once. I always keep the lights on."

Kelly nodded, like she understood this too.

Hell, she probably did.

She seemed to understand everything else.

"It hurts when you lose someone you love," she said. "Whether they leave you or they're taken from you, you're never really the same."

"Like losing your friend Ford?" Oliver asked delicately.

Kelly smiled weakly, but held back tears, her face strong. Oliver sensed—*knew*—she was a tough bitch, but still struggled with the past, that even the toughest, strongest people carried painful backstories.

"I never read your book," he said. "I couldn't, not after I heard it had the Fontaine in it."

"I understand. It's a tough read."

"Small world though, huh? We both have ugly memories of that shithole motel."

They smiled, but didn't laugh.

The world *was* small—two Michigan kids with violently-linked pasts sharing cold fries in nowhere Tennessee proved that—but not so small that either of them believed it was entirely coincidental.

Oliver, ever the optimist and eternal dreamer, wanted to believe in fate, not coincidence, like maybe this beautiful stranger was brought to him not just to deliver sad news about an FBI agent, but to be his friend or for them to help each other somehow.

"I can't believe your friends . . . *died* there, at the Fontaine." Oliver shrugged, hoping he hadn't hit a raw nerve. "Tell me about Ford."

Kelly absentmindedly dug her fingernails into the Styrofoam coffee cup. Oliver sensed he'd asked too much. Maybe it still hurt Kelly to talk about her dead friend, even after so many years.

"I'm sorry. We don't have to talk about him," he said.

Kelly cracked a softer smile and said, "I love talking about him. If I talk about him and tell people what a fucking unicorn he was, they won't remember him as a footnote in some crime story." Her smile went from soft to vibrant. "Ford was *beautiful* and funny and charming and shy and a *beefcake*. Goddamn he was pretty! I mean, we're talking Jason Patric in *The Lost Boys* kind of hot."

They laughed, but Oliver knew it was a defense. Kelly protected herself from revisiting pain by cracking jokes, just like he and Char had done for years. But those tactics wouldn't work here, not between two strangers who already understood each other better than most.

Kelly's laugh drifted and she stared through the foggy window to the outside storm and her eyes wandered, as if losing herself in her memories, just like Oliver.

"What happened at the Fontaine changed everything," Kelly said. "I didn't just lose Ford. I lost my life with him, I lost everything I believed about my friends Berger and Fawn, and I lost Jill and Matty for a year while they served time. The happy small town Norman Rockwell bubble I'd lived in my whole life burst."

"What did you do?"

"I slept a lot and ate a shitload of donuts."

They laughed and the tension eased again.

"And then I grieved, for Ford and my old life."

"*How?*"

"I couldn't let it go, so I learned to let it *be*. The grief has never left me, but I've allowed my life to grow around it with love and happiness, so it's all a part of me now."

Oliver was impressed. He'd had a difficult hospital recovery, but even more painful years spent loving and surviving Grant Carver. He wasn't sure he'd ever grieve for Grant, even though he wasn't dead, or his old life with as much grace and understanding as Kelly.

"I feel—" Oliver coughed and cleared his throat and ran his fingers through his short hair. "I feel *broken*. Not from the jump or my broken bones, but broken, like, *inside*. And I think Grant did that to me."

"You're bruised, not broken," Kelly corrected. "But even if you were, my grandmother always said, 'Broken crayons still color.'"

Oliver smiled too, *wide*. This woman really knew her shit. He felt safe and comfortable in Kelly's presence, learning her history and lessons. It confused him that they were only a year apart in age and yet Kelly was so much wiser and more put together. He wanted to be where she was, on the other side of grief, where his life could grow around it with love and happiness. Maybe he would someday. Maybe she could help. Maybe she already was.

"If we catch him—" The words felt funny and foreign rolling off Oliver's tongue. He'd never expected to say them, let alone actively pursue them. "What will happen to him?"

Kelly pulled out the thick files from her bag. When she slapped them on the tabletop, they made a thunderous BANG! louder than the outside storm. She kept her hand on top of them, as if to keep Oliver from suddenly speed-reading them faster than Johnny 5.

"Including Overstreet, Grant has killed seven that we know of," she said with a hard swallow. "Several of them were killed in death-penalty states. If he's convicted in one of those, they'll sentence him to death. Unless he cuts a deal. That's what Fawn did."

Oliver's heart skipped twice.

The authorities might kill Grant for his crimes.

The only way to stop him.

Grant.

Dead.

A world without *Grant Carver*.

Even in his darkest moments, Oliver had never considered such a world. He carried powerful residual love for Grant and always would. He'd remember the handsome leather-jacket-wearing troublemaker smoking behind the Hickory Grove High School cafeteria, and their first kiss in the Firebird's neon dashboard lights, and making love on a flannel blanket under the Oklahoma stars, and sharing a toothbrush after Grant's had fallen down the Fontaine toilet.

Eventually, Oliver hoped to remember only the good and forget the murderous madness.

But for now, Kelly was right.

Grant needed to pay for his crimes.

With his life.

Oliver respected Kelly's candor. She'd answered his questions honestly, which couldn't have been easy given the grim details, and she'd done so with compassion and plenty of humor. In another life void of Grant and Fawn and the Fontaine, he imagined they would've been great friends.

"I wish we were meeting under different circumstances," he said.

Kelly smiled. "Me too."

Oliver sighed with content. He'd told Kelly more in one greasy evening than his current therapist had heard after months of sessions. Her understanding and acceptance made him feel fearless. He couldn't remember the last time he'd felt that way.

And that fearlessness brought courage.

He pointed to the thick folders and said, "Tell me about Grant."

KELLY

They arrived in Michigan just after six a.m. and immediately crashed at Kelly's childhood home—the paper trail from examining Overstreet's files still spider-webbed in her old bedroom—but they slept only a few hours, eager to get to All Access Storage first thing.

Although weary of what might be in the storage unit, they were anxious to potentially find clues or leads or *something* that might help catch Grant, and after a brief argument over who was Sherlock in this scenario (Kelly won; Oliver had to be Watson), they entered the rental office, dressed in thick winter jackets and hats and gloves and scarves and every damn warm item Kelly found at her mother's house to help them survive the god-awful winter weather.

An elderly man sat behind a metal desk. A small black and white television with tin foil rabbit ears played a *Bonanza* rerun at full volume. The room smelled like stale cigarette smoke and day-old hot dogs, and its walls were plastered in taxidermied deer heads and a Sports Illustrated swimsuit calendar dated 1978.

"Yeah?!" A toothpick bounced between the old man's teeth.

Kelly flashed a vibrant smile. "My name's Julie Hector. This is Gillespie Armstrong. We spoke yesterday about a storage unit."

"Speak up, deary! Can't hear shit! Not since 'Nam!"

"My name's Julie! This is Gillespie! We spoke yesterday!" Kelly had shouted plenty in her youth as a back-talking loudmouth, but it felt silly and strange doing it now to a near-deaf grandfatherly shop clerk.

Art stood from the desk and shuffled over to the counter. He stared briefly at Kelly with his grey eyes and white eyebrows and she noticed he wasn't as old as she thought, maybe mid-sixties, but had clearly lived life at full throttle.

He focused closer on Oliver and asked, "You that fruit fly?!" His voice was loud, competing with an aspirin commercial on the crackly television. "Ya look differ'nt! Ya clean up yer act?"

"Yes, sir!" Oliver said loudly, as if to avoid repeating himself.

"Good! This town ain't need no fruit flies!" Art referenced a coffee-stained pad of paper with notes written in tiny scribbled handwriting Kelly couldn't read. "Unit Sixteen!" He grabbed a pair of rusty bolt cutters from under the counter. He put on a thick buffalo plaid wool coat, stepped to the door, and ordered, "Let's go!"

Kelly and Oliver smiled at each other and joined Art outside.

Art pointed to Kelly's rented BMW. "This yer car?!"

"Yes, sir!" she said.

"Let's drive!" Art opened the front passenger door and sat inside.

Kelly laughed. She liked this guy. His blunt delivery and rough exterior reminded her of Berger, and who he may have become if he'd made different choices and grown old bones.

As Oliver hopped into the backseat, Kelly sat behind the wheel and started the engine.

"Down here! Take a left! Second row on the right!" Art made wide hand gestures with long boney fingers that didn't match his directions.

Kelly slowly drove past the office, into the property's maze of storage units. The main drive had several turn-offs, each with at least a dozen units in various sizes, all with bright orange rolling garage doors and large rusty gold numbers. She ignored Art's erratic gestures and merely followed the posted signs, turning left, then right.

"Here! Here!" he barked.

Kelly parked outside the largest unit in that row—Unit 16—and they stepped out of the car, back into the burning cold.

The unit's padlock was silver and shiny and looked brand new, certainly not as if it had been left hanging since 1995. Art had mentioned seeing a beatnik fruit fly—presumably Grant—just two months ago. Clearly he'd been right.

With the bolt cutters, Art snapped off the lock in one pinch and it hit the ground.

"See me for a new lock 'fore ya leave!" he said and shuffled away.

"Do you want a ride back to the office?" Kelly asked.

Art ignored her—or didn't hear her—and kept shuffling until he disappeared behind a turn at the end of the aisle.

The ground was icy and badly-salted and Kelly and Oliver stood shoulder to shoulder for balance . . . and emotional support.

They stared at the large orange door, their breath quickly dissipating into the bitter air, neither of them as eager as before to get inside.

"To be clear," Oliver said quietly. "If we find a severed head in a jar, we're getting the hell out of here."

"Agreed," Kelly said. "But at least we're dressed better than Jodie Foster, and we won't need a car jack to open this thing."

She heaved a long breath into her gloves and stepped up to the door, knowing she'd have to make the first move. She pulled the latch and lifted the door. It rattled and rolled and raised itself on a rusty track, stopping abruptly with a screech when it reached the top.

The overcast morning light flooded the large space.

Kelly had expected dust clouds and scattering rats, like in the movies when a character entered an attic or cellar, but there wasn't any of that. The space was large—ten by twenty feet, Kelly assumed—with a concrete floor, metal walls and a hanging fluorescent light overhead.

But what Kelly and Oliver noticed first was how empty it was.

No car.

No boxes piled to the ceiling.

No treasure-mapped-*X* marking the spot.

And no signs of freshly-poured concrete to cover any bodies buried under the floor.

Kelly had kept the fears to herself, but she'd half-expected to find acid barrels or bloodied pickaxes or human-sized cages or other signs of murderous behavior, like she'd seen on *Law & Order*.

There was a dried oil stain on the concrete, presumably from where Grant's Firebird had been parked so many years ago, and two large cardboard boxes sitting on top a two-drawer filing cabinet in the rear left corner.

"This is it?" Oliver asked, his voice a unique mix of partly relieved and partly annoyed.

"Let's just be glad there isn't a refrigerator stocked with body parts," Kelly said.

"What do you think is in those boxes?" Oliver's hands were firmly tucked inside his jacket, as if to keep them from shaking.

Kelly flicked on the overhead light. "Only one way to find out." She walked to the rear of the unit, her hard-soled boots echoing loudly.

Oliver didn't move. He hadn't even entered yet, his toes just touching the inch-high lip of the unit's floor from the outside drive.

"What's wrong?" Kelly asked.

"Should we be doing this?" he asked. "We don't have a warrant—"

"Who the hell are you, *Perry Mason*? We can worry about technicalities later."

"I don't want to illegally obtain something that'll get thrown out in court and help Grant get away with what he's done."

"They have enough on him already, even without anything we find in here," she reassured. "Anything in here will only be the cherry on top of an ironclad case against him."

Oliver nodded sincerely, as if he understood and was ready to start. He stepped into the unit and stood close to Kelly.

The cardboard boxes were unmarked and appeared new with crisp edges, its flaps folded neatly with no creases, as if they'd been folded once and abandoned.

Kelly kept a wide stance from the first box, just in case Gwyneth Paltrow's head was stuffed inside, while Oliver clung to her arms, peering over her shoulder.

Kelly flipped open the box tops in one quick flick.

No head.

Inside were thick stacks of various-sized loose papers, three hardcover books—a Chet Baker biography and two jazz music histories—and four well-worn spiral-bound notebooks.

Kelly took the notebooks and handed Oliver the hardcovers.

"He loves jazz . . ." Oliver said, echoing himself from the day before. He flipped through the books' pages, looking for possible ciphers and underlined passages and everything else he'd learned from Agatha Christie novels.

Kelly did the same with the notebooks, although it was much harder to read. Grant had bad penmanship, much of it undecipherable. Most of the pages were dated 1994 or 1995 and filled with bad poetry and geometry class notes and pretty good pencil drawings of a young Oliver, which Kelly shielded from Oliver's view.

The loose paper stack was an odd combination of all kinds of miscellaneous things: old tear-outs from muscle car magazines, work schedules from Grant's afterschool job at a Flint bodyshop, junkyard invoices for car parts. But there were no handwritten confessions or red flags pointing to Grant's guilt or current location, nothing that screeched the metaphorical needle to a halt.

Until . . .

Near the bottom of the stack, tucked inside an old copy of the Metro Times, was an email printout of a rental agreement for another large storage unit in California—Simply Storage—dated October 2003.

"He has another one," Kelly said with a faster heartbeat.

"Another what?"

"Storage unit, in California. El Segundo is only twenty minutes from his Marina del Rey apartment. Maybe he has them scattered all over the place?"

"Well, if you think that's fucking weird, look at *this*."

Oliver flipped the thickest hardcover book upside down and two envelopes fell out of its pages.

"What're those?" Kelly asked.

Oliver grabbed them from the floor and handed them to Kelly.

"I think you know," he said.

Kelly took the crinkled envelopes. They were postmarked to a Hickory Grove post office box, addressed to Chet Baker. That didn't surprise Kelly, but the return address made her chest seize like she'd suddenly forgotten how to breathe.

FAWN SCHULTZ, with her name and inmate number and prison address, handwritten in pencil, just like her letters to Jill and Matt.

But these were to Grant.

Fawn had sent letters to *Grant*.

"What the fuck?" Kelly asked.

The envelopes had been opened with clean, sharp slices.

Kelly pulled out the first letter, dated June 3, 2005, just two weeks before Oliver and Grant had reunited at the high school reunion.

> *Chet!*
>
> *I can't believe you've kept everything hidden from him all these years. You really are a professional, or he's an idiot. But you'd never fall for an idiot, I suppose. Wouldn't it be more fun to tell him though? Don't you want him to know who you really are? Maybe he'd join you. Berger was eager to join me. BUT I know keeping secrets is sexy. It was so hot and dangerous and <u>exciting</u> when my friends didn't have a fucking clue.*
>
> *I hope you see him again.*
>
> *Let me know how it goes!*
>
> *xoxo*
>
> *—Fawn*

Kelly read the letter silently, although in her head she heard Fawn's voice on every goddamn word. It alarmed her how quickly she could remember Fawn's soft, wispy inflections, even after nearly ten years of not seeing or speaking to her.

She read the next letter, dated two weeks after Oliver had jumped from Grant's balcony.

July 1, 2005

I'm so sorry, Chet.
I know how much you loved him.
He wouldn't have died if O.S.
hadn't gotten involved.

That's something to think about . . .

With love,

—Fawn

In both letters, Fawn wrote cryptically, knowing her letters would be read by prison officials. Chet was obviously Grant, and the *he* Fawn referred to was presumably Oliver.

But who the hell was *O.S.*?

How was he involved in Oliver's—

Kelly's heart jackhammered her ribcage.

O.S.

*Over*Street.

Frank Overstreet.

Elusively, Fawn had planted the seed—or helped it grow—for Grant to kill Frank Overstreet.

Kelly burned hot with rage. She stood, stripped off her jacket, and paced the unit.

Oliver took the letters from her hands and read them.

Then read them again.

And a third time.

"Well, this is . . . a twist," he said. "And fucked up."

"Why the *fuck* is she corresponding with Grant?" Kelly snapped.

Oliver's eyes widened at Kelly's quick fury. "You're asking *me*? I'm Tori Spelling in *Mother, May I Sleep with Danger*, remember? I didn't have a fucking *clue* who Grant really was, so I couldn't even *begin* to guess why one killer would penpal another."

Kelly pulled off her wool cap and her dark hair fell over her face. She hooked it behind her ears.

"There's one way to find out, though," Oliver said carefully.

"What do you mean?"

Oliver licked his lips, as if to prepare his mouth for his own words, "If Fawn knows where he is . . . would she tell you?"

Kelly's stomach lurched and she stopped pacing. She'd dressed as Clarice Starling once for Halloween, complete with a shoulder-padded power suit and bob wig and Ford straight-jacketed on a dolly, but she'd never once considered—even with her wildly active imagination—her life would parallel one of her favorite movie characters.

"You can't be serious," she said to Oliver. "How much more *Silence of the Lambs* can this shit get? I'm not going to some glass-windowed jail cell so Fawn can Hannibal Lecter me."

"Uh, if you think I *want* to suggest that, you're misreading my face," Oliver clarified. He took a breath, as if to refocus or soften a verbal punch. "Do you even know where she is, what prison?"

Kelly squeezed her hands in and out of fists to burn energy. "She was moved to Chowchilla in ninety-nine. It's a women's prison about five hours outside L.A."

"She's been that close to you all this time?"

Kelly's jaw clenched. She'd done pretty well ignoring Fawn's proximity to her over the years, but it seemed ridiculously convenient now.

And potentially useful.

"Have you ever heard from her?" Oliver asked.

Kelly thought of the letters she'd stashed in the old shoebox, not a single one addressed to her. "No. Never."

"Do you think she'd talk to you?"

"I don't know. Probably? I doubt she has anything to say though."

"Might be worth a shot," Oliver said gently, as if tiptoeing around the razor wire surrounding this conversation. "Do you think you could even get in to see her?"

Overstreet had told Kelly years ago that she, Jill and Matt were on Fawn's visitation list. Kelly wasn't sure if the list was permanent and she'd never wanted to find out, but even if the list had changed, Kelly was certain Felix could arrange a visit.

But Kelly didn't want to do it.

She didn't want to *think* about it.

"Can we just keep looking, please?" she said, pointing back to the boxes and paper stacks and anything else to change direction.

Oliver shrugged in surrender and went back to digging and sorting and avoiding with Kelly.

The second box held more paperwork and keepsakes—envelopes and books and invoices and receipts and maps and vinyl records—that made no sense to either Kelly or Oliver.

"Why the hell did Grant keep all this shit?" he asked. "Why wouldn't he destroy it or burn it or *something*?"

"You need Sigourney in *Copycat* to answer that question," Kelly said with an uncertain shrug. "Maybe they're his mementos or reminders of his life and crimes, or he's just a fucking packrat. I don't know."

She tugged on the the filing cabinet drawers, but they didn't open.

Oliver smiled. "Is this the part where you pick a lock with a stolen paperclip like Sarah Connor?"

"Very funny, Dr. Silberman. Just hold it still."

Oliver steadied the top of the cabinet with both hands while Kelly jerked and yanked the bottom handle. On the fourth pull, the drawer popped open. Inside was yet another thick stack of neatly-sorted papers, and a metal *Knight Rider* lunchbox in colorful pristine condition.

Kelly handed Oliver the papers and opened the lunchbox.

Inside were two cassette tapes labeled BADASS JAZZ and SEVENTIES SHIT, a faded postcard of a mohawked Robert De Niro in *Taxi Driver*, old concert tickets, used paintbrushes, expired condoms, a crinkled pack of Marlboro Reds, and other miscellaneous sentimental garbage.

But buried at the bottom were three United States passports rubber-banded together. Kelly unbound them and opened one . . .

And saw Grant Carver's face.

He looked different than the 1995 disposable camera shots Kelly had seen, but it was him. Older, with a thicker neck but still handsome, the almost-black eyes undeniably Grant's. Sinister and sexy and shark-like, the eyes held a stern stare on the page.

Kelly checked the name.

BILLY FITZGERALD

The passport was in-date and signed in thick black ink.

She quickly checked the next passport.

Same picture.

Different name.

MILES ELLINGTON

Also in-date, also signed in the fake name.

The third passport.

DUKE HOLIDAY

Same picture, in-date, signed.

"Well, he's got guts," Kelly said, handing the passports to Oliver.

He checked each one, his eyes wide and nervous, and said, "And he's sticking with the jazz-themed aliases." He quickly handed them back to Kelly, as if they'd burned his fingers, too hot or too *scary* to hold. "Why the hell did he leave these in here?"

Kelly couldn't spot any flaws in the bogus passports. They'd clearly been forged by a professional, but Kelly was surprised Grant hadn't been more discreet. All the aliases were derived from well-known jazz greats—Dizzie Gillespie, Louis Armstrong, Billie Holiday, Ella Fitzgerald, Miles Davis, Duke Ellington and, of course, Chet Baker—with no obscurity or originality.

Kelly had learned from Fawn and Berger that killers could hide in plain sight. Grant Carver clearly was no different, and that casualness and arrogance scared the hell out of her.

She rechecked the Simply Storage rental agreement in El Segundo. It had been rented under the name Miles Ellington.

"How do you even get a fake passport?" Oliver asked. "Don't you need Q from *James Bond* for that sort of shit?"

Kelly dug through the other items in the lunchbox, trying to find a connection, some reason why intricately-made passports were just thrown in with sentimental mementos. But she only found more memory lane bullshit—Soundgarden concert tickets, a Pearl Jam pin, an old report card (mostly D's), and movie ticket stubs.

"This is so wacky," she said. "He just left fake passports in an old lunchbox with mixtapes and fucking tickets to Dino's Drive-In?"

Oliver dropped a stack of papers; it scattered around his feet. "What did you just say?"

"Dino's." Kelly held the stubs into the light to read the fading text. "A *Pulp Fiction* and *Wes Craven's New Nightmare* double-feature."

In one quick swipe, Oliver ripped off his hat and peeled off his scarf, gasping for air, his face white and frozen, like he'd just seen Freddy Krueger himself.

"What's wrong with you?" she asked. "Why do you look like Carrie just set fire to the gym with her brain?"

Oliver's eyes watered and his entire body shook. He slowly held out his hand and Kelly gave him the ticket stubs. He read them and released a soft cry.

Kelly stepped over the scattered papers and hugged his shoulders. "*Pulp Fiction* was good, but not cry-worthy good."

"These are from our first date," Oliver whispered. "We had our first kiss that night. It was my first kiss *ever*."

Kelly smiled. She'd kept childhood pictures and birthday cards from Fawn—snapshots of their unspoiled youth—that still tugged Kelly's heartstrings whenever she'd look at them, so she understood Oliver's sudden nostalgia. Regardless of the way their relationships had ended with Grant and Fawn, they'd started pure and sincere and magical, and hanging on to the early parts—the good stuff—made the aftermath a *little* more bearable.

Kelly kissed Oliver's temple and said, "Keep 'em."

Oliver nodded but didn't speak . . . and slipped the tickets into the inside pocket of his jacket, right next to his heart.

Kelly knelt to the floor and gathered the scattered papers. There were old paychecks from the Flint bodyshop, a few unpaid Consumers Energy bills for Grant's father's house, and a two deposit receipts from something called Parkland Greene, which Kelly had never heard of and the receipts had no identifying business information.

Beneath those papers was a glassy full-color brochure for a Canadian video production studio called Otturatore, with several internet printouts for the same company stapled to it. The brochure detailed various production services and praising testimonials from high-profile customers. On the back was a black and white photograph of a beautiful olive-skinned late-twentysomething man, the company's owner and head video director. The attached printouts included a list of the man's producing credentials and resume, and driving directions from Seattle to the studio's Vancouver street address.

"Have you ever heard of Otturatore?" Kelly asked. "Looks like a production house in Canada."

Oliver didn't answer.

Still kneeling, Kelly glanced at him.

His ghostly-white face from moments earlier remained, only now he was less surprised and more scared.

Terrified.

Kelly stood up quickly and asked, "What is it?"

"What did you say?" Oliver whispered.

Kelly flashed the brochure. "*Otturatore.* Shit, my Italian's awful."

"In Vancouver?" Oliver asked, his eyes flooded. "On The Drive?"

"Says it's 'in the heart of everything on Commercial Drive.' Why?"

Tears ran down Oliver's face.

His knees shook, but not from the cold, from *fear*.

"Oliver, what's wrong?"

"That's Giancarlo's studio," he said, barely speaking.

"Who's Giancarlo? And why do you look like Jack Nicholson is trying to chop down your bathroom door?"

Kelly reread the brochure's brief bio of the pictured Italian man.

GIANCARLO OSSANI, 29. Positano, Italy. Owner/Head Director

"You know this Italian Stallion?" she asked.

Oliver held his shaking hand over his mouth, as if to prevent himself from releasing a wounded cry or terrified scream.

"Oliver?"

He shook his head, as if unable to find words . . . or the bravery to speak them.

"Oh, now you're Holly Hunter in *The Piano*? You can't speak? Oliver, goddammit! *What*?"

"He loved me," Oliver whispered. "And I almost loved him back."

Kelly's heart sank.

Love.

She hadn't considered Oliver might have an ex. He'd spent a decade chasing after Grant Carver and she'd assumed that hadn't left any time for anyone else. And yet, from the scared-shitless look on Oliver's teary face, Giancarlo had mattered, *a lot*.

Kelly pointed to Giancarlo's picture and asked, "You and this hunky babe were a thing?"

Oliver's nodded and swallowed and said, "We met on a video shoot. He was directing and I was hired to take some publicity shots. And, well . . . if sparks are real, we lit up like the Fourth of July. He was—*is*—beautiful and smart and funny and kind and—"

"*And*?"

Oliver smiled and shrugged and seemed to lose himself for a minute; remembering had a way of doing that, Kelly had learned.

"We were together for two years and it was perfect. *He* was perfect," he said. "We were really happy, travelling the world for work and making love and just being together." He wiped his face with his jacket sleeve. "But I couldn't love him back, not the way he deserved."

"Because of Grant?"

Oliver nodded and cried. He seemed suddenly overwhelmed and scared, all at once. He paced the concrete, his breathing quick, shaking his hands, as if to burn off energy or keep them from striking the wall. His mind was beyond memories, Kelly could tell, and far into potentially grim future scenarios.

"Why does Grant have Giancarlo's information?" Oliver's voice lost went from whisper to fiery panic. "*Why*? Why would he have this?"

Oliver stopped pacing and looked at Kelly.

Instantly, they connected the dots.

And Kelly's heart skipped two beats.

"He wants to kill Giancarlo!" Oliver shrieked.

"Hang on! We don't know—"

Oliver snatched the papers out of Kelly's hands and quickly flipped through them, furiously wiping away tears as he read.

"I've seen enough episodes of *Criminal Intent* to know what you're thinking," Kelly said. "But we don't know anything for sure—"

"Fuck, Kelly! Why else would he have this?! He wants to kill *another* person I care about!"

"Oliver—"

"Ohmygod! Maybe he already has! Did he kill him?! Is Giancarlo dead?! Are we too late?!"

Kelly squeezed Oliver's arms *hard*. "Calm down, Shirley MacLaine. The doctor will bring your daughter's pills. Now take a breather and let me make a call before we panic."

She led Oliver to the corner and sat him on the file cabinet. She opened her Razr and dialed the Canadian telephone number on the front of the Otturatore brochure.

"*Ciao*! Otturatore Studios. This is Sofia. How may I help you?"

"Hi, Sofia. My name is Kelly Garrett. I work for the Townsend Agency in Los Angeles—" Whenever in need of strength, Kelly's go-to was a *Charlie's Angels* reference. "I'm interested in hiring Giancarlo Ossani for a perfume campaign my agency is handling. Is he in the office today? I like to speak with him directly."

"I'm terribly sorry, Ms. Garrett, but Mr. Ossani is currently out of the country on sabbatical and unavailable."

"When is he scheduled to return?"

"I'm afraid I cannot disclose that information."

"How long has he been gone?"

"Since June. Would you like his voicemail?"

"Does he check messages? When did you last speak to him?"

"Yes, he does. I spoke to him yesterday afternoon. I could also connect you with our consulting department. I'm sure you'd be pleased with our other experienced directors and staff for your campaign—"

"No, thank you. Just Mr. Ossani's voicemail."

"Of course. One moment."

A muzak rendition of Madonna's *Live to Tell* played briefly before a deep, Italian-accented voice said, "You've reached Giancarlo Ossani. You know what to do. *Grazie*."

After the beep, Kelly spoke casually but firmly, "My name is Kelly Spencer. I need to speak with you regarding Oliver Foster. It's very important. Please call me as soon as you get this." She rattled off her mobile number and hung up.

"*Well*?" Oliver asked, his arms folded tightly against himself.

"He's been out of the country since June," Kelly said. "The receptionist said she spoke to him yesterday. He's alive."

Oliver stared at her, his face wet and tired, his eyes heavy and scared. "Kelly, I—"

Kelly held his hand. "We'll find him."

"What if Grant . . . kills him?"

Kelly wouldn't promise Oliver anything she couldn't deliver. She didn't know if Giancarlo was alive or dead and appeasing Oliver with empty sentiments or false assurances would be cruel.

So she squeezed his fingers and said, "We'll find him either way."

Oliver rolled his eyes. "*How*?"

"I have a handsome FBI agent up my sleeve. Felix will find him."

"What about Grant?"

Kelly pointed to Fawn's letters. "Let's start there."

Oliver nodded, as if understanding her intention, and sat up straight. He wiped his face and said "I'll go with you, back to L.A."

Kelly didn't immediately dismiss the idea, but said, "If Grant's still in L.A., it might be dangerous for you to be there."

Oliver took the ticket stubs out of his pocket. Without looking at them, he tossed them back into the lunchbox and said, "It's different now. It's not just about me. I have to save Giancarlo. I *have* to."

Kelly knew that look—the determined yet petrified stare. She'd had it herself once, after learning the truth of Fawn and Berger's lies and manipulation, and probably again after seeing Grant Carver's name for the first time.

"I can't keep Giancarlo safe if I'm living like Julia Roberts in *Sleeping with the Enemy*, tucked away in some fake Chattanooga life," Oliver said. "I want my real life back and I want to save his. If we have to risk everything in L.A., let's do it. I've lost enough. We both have."

"That's a hell of a speech," Kelly said.

And it was.

Kelly was inspired and dialed Felix's long protocol number.

"Are you okay?" he asked after a single ring.

"We're both fine," she said. "I need some help."

"Of course."

Kelly smiled as his unquestioning support. "Simply Storage in El Segundo. Check for a unit rented under the name Miles Ellington."

She heard pen scratching on paper. Felix was taking notes in his bold, hard strokes.

"Who is that?" he asked.

"One of Grant's aliases."

"*One*? How many are there?"

"A few."

"How do you know that?"

"That's a long story. I'll tell you later." Kelly didn't want to lose the momentum and added, "If I give you the names, can you run them?"

"Of course."

Kelly spoke them slowly so Felix could write them down, then said, "I need you to send local agents to All Access Storage in Hickory Grove, Michigan. They'll need to process this storage unit. I've got a P.O. box for you to trace too."

"Is that where you are now, a storage unit?"

"Yes. I need you to find someone too."

"Who?"

"His name is Giancarlo Ossani. He owns a production company in

Vancouver." She rattled off Otturatore's telephone number and address plus a mobile number Oliver had remembered but was disconnected. "We think he might be Grant's next target."

Pen scratching came fierce and fast through the phone. "Got it," Felix said. "I'll find him. Anything else?"

Kelly absentmindedly ran her fingernail along the frayed edge of a cardboard box, stalling.

"Kelly? Are you there?"

"Yes, I'm here."

"What's wrong?"

"There's one more thing," she whispered.

"Anything."

Kelly took a breath to calm her heart and went for it, "Can you get me in to see Fawn?"

The line went silent briefly, then Felix asked, "Are you sure?"

Kelly nodded, even though he couldn't see her.

She was sure; scared shitless, but sure.

"Yes," she said. "Can you get me in?"

"I can get you visitation, yes," Felix said.

"Okay. Thanks." Kelly cleared her throat to chase away any lingering doubts or fears. "I'm bringing Oliver back to L.A. with me. Can you arrange for an agent to fly with us for his safety?"

"Yes."

"Thank you, Felix."

"Kelly . . . how did you find all this?

"We're following the breadcrumbs. Guess I'm back on carbs."

Felix laughed, although Kelly could sense it was partly forced, as if he was more worried than relieved at her success and the danger of inching closer to a killer. Worrying was part of his job, but he'd never had to worry about Kelly before. She knew he was scared, but his razor-sharp focus would help mask his fears.

"We're safe," she assured. "I'll see you soon."

"I'll book your flights with an accompanying agent," he said, already focused on action. "I'll call you back once I have the information. Stay at the storage unit until agents arrive. I'll send them now."

"Thank you."

"I miss you, Kel."

Kelly smiled. He loved her and she loved him. They'd never used that word, but it was *understood*, especially in moments like this, when he missed her or she wanted to hear his voice before she slept.

"I miss you too, Felix. Call me back." She hung up.

"*Well*?" Oliver asked,

"He's on it," Kelly said. "And he's sending agents to meet us here."

Oliver exhaled a long sigh that puffed his cheeks. "Good. After they get here and before I completely freak the fuck out and loose my mind over all this trail of tears we've uncovered, can we get a goddamn drink? I don't give a shit that it's only lunchtime."

Kelly clapped her hands once and cheered, "Ohmygodyes!"

KELLY & OLIVER

Kelly and Oliver went to Venus—*Penis*—Coney Island, which had somehow landed a liquor license and banned smoking since they'd last visited so many years ago. They drank weak whiskey-cokes and ate French fries. Oliver reminisced about his magical two years with Giancarlo Ossani, while Kelly swooned over the fiercely supportive and devoted Felix Macallum.

After eating and drinking and gushing about boys, they sobered and discussed everything they'd found in Grant's storage unit. They'd been granted photocopies of a few documents by the on-site FBI agents processing the scene—Grant's fake passports, the El Segundo rental agreement, and the Otturatore brochure.

After lunch, they visited their old local haunts: Hickory Grove and Isaac High Schools, both built up and extended since they'd been students there; Oliver's childhood home on Hogan Road, lush and loved by the young couple who'd bought it from his parents; Dino's Drive-In, now an empty parking lot with only its street sign remaining; St. John's church, where Ford's funeral had been held, still bricked and beautiful; and Grant's old house, where he'd murdered his father, now abandoned and graffitied and overgrown with tall grass.

So much of both towns had changed since they'd last been there, even since June when Oliver had attended his ten year reunion. He and Kelly felt like outsiders, aliens crash-landed into someone else's life.

Felix worked fast on investigating Kelly's leads: the Hickory Grove post office had no paper trail for the P.O. box Fawn had used, other than Grant had used his dead father's old abandoned house address as its backup; Giancarlo Ossani was scheduled to land in New York City that evening and Felix had two agents scheduled to escort him to Los

Angeles; a storage unit rented in El Segundo under the name Miles Ellington was discovered, with a search warrant pending; and a search on Fawn's prison cell for any possible correspondence with Grant Carver came up empty, nothing but accounting textbooks, old photographs of herself with Berger, and a well-worn copy of Tarantino's *Natural Born Killers* screenplay. If she'd ever received letters from Grant, she'd clearly destroyed them.

Felix made sure to run searches on every cell in Fawn's block, so she wouldn't suspect any singling out, even though no one particularly cared if she suspected anything or not. But if she had ways of contacting Grant, they had to remain vigilante and one step ahead. And Felix demanded monitoring of Fawn's further communications—telephone calls and all incoming and outgoing mail.

Kelly and Oliver spent the evening at Kelly's childhood home again. And after a surprisingly comfortable sleep—exhaustion had a way of doing that too—Kelly and Oliver, accompanied by a Felix-chosen FBI agent, flew to Los Angeles.

To get back to work.

And to finish what they'd started.

OLIVER

WEDNESDAY, DECEMBER 7, 2005
12:06 PM PST

When Oliver and Kelly arrived at her home, a broad, handsome hunk with a shaved head opened the door. His eyes lit up brighter than the Christmas lights strung on nearby palms trees when he saw Kelly. She hugged him and they kissed. He held on tight to her and closed his eyes, as if he'd been worried, now relieved she was home safely.

"Oliver, this is Felix," Kelly said.

"You're really not a cartoon! Or a clock!" Oliver laughed.

Oliver should've known this powerhouse was Kelly's boyfriend. Such a beautiful woman would only date an equally-beautiful man.

"She's still using that lame joke about my name, I see." Felix shook Oliver's hand. "Please come in."

Felix took their bags and Kelly led them inside. The house was large and open and colored in whites and blues and greens and smelled like fresh strawberries and peppermint. Kelly showed Oliver to a large ocean-facing bedroom at the end of a long hallway.

"You can stay in here," she said. "As long as you need."

She flicked on the light and the room was designed straight out of Architectural Digest or an exclusive beachside resort showpiece. There were even freshly fluffed and folded bath towels and two chocolate mints on an oversized bed. Kelly was one hell of a host.

"Let's order Chinese and talk to Felix, if you're up to it," Kelly said.

"That sounds great," Oliver said and meant it. He felt safe here, not just because there was an FBI agent in the house and two more in unmarked cars outside and probably more patrolling the beach if Felix was as overprotective as Kelly claimed, but because Kelly felt like more than a stranger or casual acquaintance. After everything they'd discussed, he trusted her. They made a good team.

They ate Chinese food for lunch and drank wine and sat around the softly-lit live Christmas tree Felix had decorated in the living room while Kelly was gone, and they told Felix everything they'd discovered in Michigan, although the Hickory Grove storage unit was now being fine-tooth-combed by the FBI for anything they might have missed.

Felix lectured Oliver on the seriousness of leaving witness protection and made calls to update the proper departments on Oliver's current location and security; and he insisted Oliver remain inside Kelly's home for his safety until Grant was apprehended. Oliver understood, of course, and appreciated Felix's unique delivery. He was authoritative, but kind. Oliver didn't have many memories of Frank Overstreet since he'd been so distraught and unhinged during those few brief meetings in 1995, but Oliver remembered his kindness. Oliver could see why Kelly was attracted to Felix. He was a lot like the fallen agent.

As the night went on, Oliver relaxed. Relaxation was easy in such a beautiful place. He and Giancarlo had lived together in a Vancouver high-rise and later in a small Positano flat on the Tyrrhenian Sea. The views from those homes were spectacular, but the vast blue Pacific in front of Kelly's Barbie Dream House was hard to beat. Even in the dark, moonlight reflecting off the waves, it was soothing and spectacular.

This same ocean, nearly this same view from Grant's Marina del Rey apartment only a matter of miles down the beach, had been the last thing Oliver saw before jumping six months ago. He'd unrealistically hoped to jump into the water from that balcony, fully knowing he'd plummet to his death on the concrete below instead.

But he hadn't died; he'd *survived*.

Yet here he was again, mere miles from that apartment under very different circumstances, with a strong, determined woman hell-bent on getting him his life back.

They sat on the living room couch with the back door open, drinking wine and filling in blanks and listening to the waves lap the shore.

When the doorbell rang, Oliver jumped a little and laughed.

"I invited some friends over," Kelly said. "Don't worry."

After a long morning of flying and fighting L.A. traffic and a long afternoon of rehashing his past, Oliver wasn't in the mood. "Can we do it another time? I'm tired."

"You'll want to see them. Trust me."

Kelly left the living room.

Oliver heard the front door open.

Moments later, a little blonde boy aged four or five—dressed in designer jeans and a Beatles T-shirt—ran up to the couch and jumped onto the cushion beside Oliver.

"Hiiiii!" the boy said with a huge smile and tiny teeth.

Oliver laughed and said, "Hey, little man!"

Oliver looked up from the beautiful boy and saw a beautiful long-haired blonde woman with perfect porcelain skin and a warm smile. She was about his age and somehow Oliver just knew she was Jillian George, Kelly's best friend.

But Oliver paid little attention to her.

Instead, his eyes deadlocked on the tall, broad, strawberry-blonde-bearded man standing beside her. The man smiled and Oliver was certain he was hallucinating.

After jumping from Grant's balcony, he'd been on heavy painkillers and sedatives to ease his broken body and his troubled mind. The powerful drugs had caused disorienting yet realistic visions—a 1994-Marky Mark dropping trou while standing on a giant stethoscope, a *Pump-Up-the-Volume*-era Christian Slater DJing into a giant cigarette—that had been merely vivid hallucinations.

And it was happening again, only sober.

Because it couldn't actually be *Nate* standing before him.

Nate, the handsome Southern gentleman who'd worked the front desk at the Fontaine Motel; the man who'd dried and dressed Oliver after he'd wandered into the pouring rain after Grant had abandoned him in the middle of the night; the man who'd put Oliver on a bus to Chicago to get him the hell out of that middle of nowhere and back to Char; the man who'd given kindness and compassion to a stranger when he'd needed it most.

Oliver remembered all the in-depth chats he'd had with Kelly over the last few days and her mentioning Jill and Nate were married, but it hadn't really registered with Oliver, not until he laid eyes on Nate again, that it was real, that he might actually see him again himself.

"Howdy, Oliver." Nate had the same deep, slow Southern drawl.

Oliver hadn't forgotten. Even after jumping toward death and breaking his bones and his heart and nearly knocking the brains out of his skull, Oliver *remembered* Nate's voice.

"Nate?"

Oliver's mouth was terribly dry and his throat burned. He was going to cry. He'd done that a lot lately, but this was different. This was charged with relief and surprise and *joy*.

Nate smiled and said, "Oliver Twist."

Oliver released a cry-laugh.

Oliver Twist.

Oliver had written the alias in the Fontaine Motel's registry ledger. Nate had known it was faked, but he'd played along for the thrill of

Oliver and Grant's road trip adventure. Oliver had forgotten that, until this handsome ghost from his past spoke it again.

Oliver slowly stood from the couch. Nate met him in the center of the room and quickly took Oliver in his arms and held him close.

"It's real good to see you again," Nate said quietly.

Oliver hugged him back, *tight*, and allowed himself to cry on Nate's shoulder. Nate winced a little, probably decade-old discomfort in his left shoulder from being shot with Fawn's gun at the Fontaine. Oliver knew better than anyone that old wounds had a habit of lingering longer than necessary.

Nate smelled the same, like smoke and wintergreen breath mints, and in an instant Oliver was eighteen again, standing in the pouring rain, barefoot in the muddy Fontaine parking lot, with Nate's protective arm slung over his shoulder. Oliver hadn't had clarity then to recognize or appreciate Nate's care, but he'd thought of it a lot since.

"I've never forgotten your kindness," Oliver whispered. "You saved my life that night."

"You just needed some help," Nate said, his deep voice reverberating through Oliver's bones, just like it had that night in the rain. "I wish I could've done more, 'cuz I ain't never forgotten you neither."

Nate's accent was still pronounced, but softer than Oliver recalled. Maybe a decade in California had changed it. Or maybe he'd changed.

"I just wish I, uh—" Nate couldn't find the words, accented or not.

Oliver stepped back from their embrace to look at Nate's handsome face. "What is it?"

Nate shrugged, as if unsure how to articulate his feelings. "I wish I'd known you were so close, you know, before you jumped."

Oliver smiled, touched by this rugged gent's protective instincts, and said, "There's nothing you could've done."

"I should've done somethin' then, at the motel. I saw him before he ran out on you. I should've wrangled him into stayin' or somethin'."

In the ten years since waking up alone in the neon darkness of Room 10 at the Fontaine Motel, Oliver had never thought there might be a witness to his abandonment, that Nate might've seen or heard something, possibly even a reason why Grant had left him.

"You saw him before he left?" Oliver asked.

Nate nodded. "He came to the office before the rain poured."

"Did he say anything?"

"He gave me a lotta money to pay for your room as long as you'd need it, and asked me to look after you, said you might need that too."

Oliver looked for Kelly and Felix, although they were nowhere to be found, presumably to give him time alone with Nate. Then Oliver glanced at the blonde he presumed to be Jill, then back to Nate. What he was looking for, he wasn't sure. Guidance? More information? An escape hatch to get him out of his memories?

"I asked if everythin' was okay," Nate added. "He almost said somethin', but only asked me not to tell anyone I'd seen him."

"Did he say where he was going?"

"No."

"Why didn't you tell me?"

"Would it have mattered?"

Oliver didn't answer.

It *wouldn't* have mattered. Grant had already left. Knowing he'd told a front desk clerk wouldn't have changed the outcome.

"How did he . . . Did he seem upset?" Oliver asked.

Nate shook his head. "He was in a hurry, I guess, but he was . . . *cool*. Level-headed. No worries or nothin'."

Oliver actually laughed.

Cool.

That was Grant all right.

Even before ditching Oliver in the middle of nowhere in the middle of the night, he was fucking cool and calm.

And a goddamn killer.

"I'm sorry for what he did to you, Oliver," Nate said. "If I'd known, I would've stopped him and saved you a whole lotta pain."

"I'm sorry for what happened to you too." Oliver wiped his face. "Kelly told me you got shot during Fawn's *True Romance* rampage."

"Ain't no need to be sorry. If it hadn't happened, I never would've met my beautiful wife."

Oliver smiled at presumably-Jill again and laughed. "Sorry! I'm a blubbering mess and we haven't even met! I'm Oliver."

"Dammit! Where're my manners?" Nate put his hand on the small of the beautiful blonde's back and said, "This here's Jill."

"Hi," she said sweetly and hugged Oliver. She smelled like oranges and sunshine.

Oliver held on to her too, tight, almost as a thank you, and said, "Your husband saved me once, when I needed it most."

A bright smile graced Jill's pretty face, like she understood all too well. "He has a knack for that." She exchanged a couple's look with Nate, loaded with hidden meanings and inside-jokes and *love*.

"And this li'l rascal—" Nate picked up the little boy, who was giggling and circling Nate's tall legs, and draped him over his shoulder. "—is our son, Li'l Ford."

Oliver's throat seized, like he might cry more tears of joy.

"It was our way of honoring Ford," Jill said, the Christmas tree lights twinkling in her wet eyes. "This way his memory will live on."

"That's beautiful," Oliver said.

Little Ford tugged Nate's beard and giggled when Nate faked pain.

"Ford, this is Mr. Oliver," Nate said. "He's a friend of Daddy's."

"Hiiiii!"

"It's very nice to meet you, little man." Oliver ruffled Little Ford's white-blonde hair.

"Did you know Uncle Ford too?"

"No, but I know he was a really cool dude, just like you."

Little Ford giggled and squirmed out of Nate's grasp. He flashed a toothy grin, waved goodbye, and ran off to play.

Oliver was suddenly so warm and exuberant. His life may have stopped at the Fontaine once, but Nate's hadn't. Or Jill's. Or Kelly's. They'd all created successful, fulfilled, incredibly *happy* lives.

In this moment, surrounded by these wonderful, kind people, that Oliver truly realized how badly he wanted his life back.

And he'd do whatever he could to get it.

OLIVER

THURSDAY, DECEMBER 8, 2005
1:19 PM PST

Oliver paced Kelly's Barbie Dream House for hours.

Giancarlo was due to land on a flight from New York that morning with FBI escorts and Felix was picking him up from the airport, but for safety reasons, Oliver hadn't been able to tag along—he couldn't even leave the house—but Kelly had, hoping to make Giancarlo's experience a little less scary.

But that had been hours ago.

Alone in the house, Oliver wandered the halls, drinking coffee and remembering his life with Giancarlo—sharing a Vancouver high-rise, cooking handmade pasta with Giancarlo's *papà* in Italy, creative work collaborations, skinny dipping in the Tyrrhenian Sea, and *love*.

The wonderful, magical memories were easy to remember.

But the heartbreaking, tragic ones were too, especially the breakup, when Oliver had been unable to give himself completely to Giancarlo because his lingering love for Grant had been too powerful and he'd chosen chasing a ghost over claiming happiness with Giancarlo.

Oliver now knew choosing Grant had been a mistake, but that crystal-clear clarity had only come after Grant's horrific crimes were exposed. Oliver couldn't change what he'd done.

And he wasn't sure if Giancarlo would want to see him again. He didn't have much of a choice since he was now under FBI protection, but that didn't mean Giancarlo would have to engage with him. Oliver had broken his heart, *badly*, and he deserved an ice-cold shoulder.

But before Oliver could dwell on too many crippling what-ifs, the front door finally opened and he ran to it.

Not only had he waited impatiently for hours, but part of him still didn't believe that this was real, that he'd actually see Giancarlo again.

And yet . . .

There he was.

The man he'd wanted but hadn't allowed himself to love once, backlit by sunshine and standing in the doorway of the Dream House.

Giancarlo Ossani.

Tall, dark and incredibly handsome, wearing expensive blue jeans that hugged all the perfectly-muscled parts and a tight plain-white T-shirt and thin blue cardigan, both stretched over his broad shoulders.

Fuck! Oliver had forgotten how beautiful he was.

But what really got him was the goddamn smile.

When Giancarlo saw Oliver, he flashed an impossibly-wide and white smile and Oliver was suddenly so happy. He knew that smile, *remembered* it.

Regardless of the circumstances—or perhaps because of them—Giancarlo was happy too, and his smile was genuine and loaded, as if he too remembered everything.

"Come in," Kelly told Giancarlo.

She and Felix had apparently entered the house first and were standing in the foyer, although Oliver hadn't noticed. He couldn't break his stare with Giancarlo's beautiful brown eyes.

Giancarlo dropped his leather shoulder bag and a vintage hard-shell green suitcase to the floor and rushed to Oliver without shutting the door. He took Oliver in his arms, gripping his hands against Oliver's ribcage then locking them at the small of Oliver's back, where they'd always just fit in their old life together.

Oliver cradled Giancarlo's neck in his elbows and buried his head onto his shoulder. He'd forgotten how strong and fit Giancarlo was—firm and full to the touch; and he smelled the same, like expensive cologne, minty-fresh toothpaste and his favorite leather camera strap.

"It's true," Giancarlo whispered. "Óliver . . . you're *alive.*"

Oliver had forgotten this too, the way Giancarlo spoke his name. Grant had always spoken it in italics, as if it was special and one-of-a-kind. Oliver never believed anyone else would handle his name with such delicate care. And yet, he'd forgotten Giancarlo had for years too, with an inexplicable circumflex, dipped in Italian-accented sexiness.

Oliver was unsettled. How hadn't he noticed the two drastically-different loves of his life had delivered his name so distinctly?

What else hadn't he noticed?

"I thought you were dead," Giancarlo whispered.

"I wanted to be," Oliver said. "But I'm here now."

Oliver felt a tiny warm splash on the back of his neck, presumably one of Giancarlo's fallen tears. Oliver kept his hands on Giancarlo's shoulders but inched back to see his handsome face. Giancarlo was crying, his cheeks and short black stubble wet with tears.

Without words or instruction, Kelly and Felix left the room, as if knowing how important—how *monumental*—this moment was for both Oliver and Giancarlo.

Giancarlo kissed Oliver's mouth, softly, with no romance or horny agenda, just relief and love, as if overwhelmed by the chance to do it again, something he'd never expected possible.

Oliver rubbed Giancarlo's wet face. The stubble tickled his fingers.

Suddenly, Oliver felt protected, truly and completely. The Dream House had been under constant 24-hour FBI protection and Oliver knew Felix and Kelly wouldn't put him in any unnecessary danger, but staring into Giancarlo's moist brown eyes, Oliver felt *safe*.

Before he'd leapt from Grant's balcony, Oliver had thought of his life with Giancarlo. Those memories had brought him comfort in what he'd thought would be his final moments. That comfort was here again, only Oliver wanted it to last this time, to catapult beyond Grant Carver and the sinister reasons he and Giancarlo had been reunited.

The day before, Oliver had realized he wanted to reclaim his life. That life could now include this beautiful Italian man from his past too and Oliver could barely stand still at the exciting prospect.

But they had a lot to discuss before any friendship—or something stronger—could rekindle.

"We couldn't find you. I was so scared that—" Oliver stopped himself, refusing to vocalize his fears. "Where have you been?"

"After you . . . *jumped*—" Giancarlo's voice broke and he swallowed hard. "I've spent the last six months searching for answers, everywhere and nowhere. I just *wandered*, through monasteries in Tibet, meditation retreats in Thailand, at the foot of the Western Wall in Jerusalem. It wasn't about religion, it was about help. I needed guidance, to know why you were taken from me, why you died."

Oliver's throat tightened. "Did you find it? *Help*?"

Giancarlo gave a weak, defeated smile. "No, *amore*. But I found peace. Maybe that's all I was supposed to find until I found you again."

Knowing Giancarlo had suffered hurt and Oliver suspected Giancarlo was faking or downplaying his newfound peace to shield him from any real, debilitating heartbreak.

"You haven't been home for six months?" Oliver asked.

"I have no home," Giancarlo said. "I sublet the Vancouver flat and left for Asia the week after you died."

Oliver released a low, relieved sigh. "That's why he couldn't find you. You were out of the country."

Giancarlo didn't ask *who*. Grant's ghost had haunted their relationship from the start, so he damn well already knew *who*.

"Why is Grant looking for me?" he asked. "To kill me?"

Tears fell from Oliver's eyes. "*Yes.*"

"Because you and I used to be together?"

Oliver nodded. "I'm so sorry."

Although his own tears fell, Giancarlo's expression didn't change and he held Oliver's hand to his heart. "*Sono felice, amore.* I'm so happy to see you. I never thought this would happen, so don't be sorry."

He kissed Oliver's knuckles and Oliver's knees bent slightly. He wasn't sure he could take any more charm. After everything—a painful breakup, years apart, a murderous ex apparently bloodthirsty for his life—Giancarlo was still happy to see him.

Oliver had a sudden urge to apologize for *everything*, but he wasn't sure how the hell to vocalize an apology for their history or his leaving or his devotion to a killer.

So he tried, "I don't know what—"

But Giancarlo quickly interrupted, as if he'd been processing it all too, "Let's not talk about any of that right now. We'll have plenty of time after he's caught."

Oliver appreciated the free-pass and shared uncertainty and hugged the beautiful Italian again, squeezing them together tightly.

Eventually, Oliver would tell Giancarlo everything—about his death-wish jump from Grant's balcony and his subsequent miraculous recovery, to Overstreet's murder, to everything he and Kelly had uncovered about Grant's lies and crimes.

And he'd ask Giancarlo about his life since they'd last seen each other—about Giancarlo's quest for peace and his professional successes and maybe even his love life. *Maybe.* Given the smile on Giancarlo's face, Oliver was pretty sure he already knew the answer to that.

And maybe they'd talk about *them*, their history and their past relationship. Giancarlo would allow Oliver the safety and comfort to express his regrets in hurting him, and Giancarlo would in turn clarify or condemn a few things.

But all that would all come later since their quiet reunion didn't need any more words, not right now.

For now, Oliver and Giancarlo stood in the foyer of the Dream House wrapped in each other's arms, gently swaying in perfect rhythm, like when they'd slow-danced to Roberta Flack records in the Positano flat in the summer of 2002.

"I have one question though," Giancarlo whispered. "Do you still sleep with the lights on?"

Oliver laughed.

Jesus, this guy remembered *everything*.

"Yes," Oliver said. "*Why?*"

"Just want to know if I'll need an eye mask later." Giancarlo playfully wagged his eyebrows.

Oliver's heart fluttered and flipped.

Giancarlo slept in complete darkness. During their relationship, he'd worn blackout eye masks to block the constant bedroom light. He'd never once complained or shamed Oliver for it, but had made occasional jokes after they'd made love about the mask's zero sexiness.

And he made light of it now, with humor and a hint of horniness, just like he always had, like nothing had changed.

And just like that, Giancarlo Ossani was back.

KELLY
FRIDAY, DECEMBER 9, 2005
10:53 AM PST

Kelly approached the sign-in counter.

The large lobby had two rows of plastic yellow chrome-legged chairs with waiting visitors and armed guards. Kelly had insisted Felix wait for her outside in his car, confident she could face prison visitation alone. And she could, but she suddenly felt very alone and afraid.

An overweight female corrections officer with chapped rosy cheeks and sky-high braided hair sat behind a sliding glass partition window, her long holiday-colored acrylic fingernails rat-a-tat-tapping on a computer keyboard.

"Can I help you, sweetie?" Her identification badge read S. RITA and featured a photograph of her flashing a wide, joyous smile.

"I'm here to see an inmate," Kelly said.

"What's your name, sweetie? Show me your I.D."

Kelly handed over her driver's license.

Rita checked the computer . . .

Then a logbook . . .

Then the computer again . . .

Then she looked back to Kelly, her wide eyes surrounded by thick black eyelash extensions, and asked, "You're here to see the Motel Murderess? For real?"

"Are you allowed to call her that?" Kelly asked.

Rita waved her festive nails in jest. "Don't take no offense, sweetie. We like to use the silly nicknames the press gives our gals whenever we can. Makes 'em seem less scary. But to the inmates she ain't the Motel Murderess. She ain't much of nothin', really 'cuz she don't talk much. Everybody calls her *Bookworm* 'cuz she always got her nose in a book."

That sounded like Fawn. She'd always loved reading *The Baby-*

Sitters Club and *Sweet Valley High* books when they were little, and proofreading and editing Kelly's early short stories and high school newspaper articles.

"What is she . . . *like*?" Kelly's heart pumped a few irregular beats. "It's been a long time since I've seen her."

"You're the first, sweetie," Rita said. "I've been here since she was transferred and she ain't never had a single visitor. You're the first."

Kelly smiled, happy to know Fawn had never been visited. She didn't deserve visitors, or the attention she craved.

"*Good*," Kelly said.

"Mmmhmmm," Rita mumbled in agreement. She handed back Kelly's license and a printed visitor's pass. "You must know someone high up too, sweetie. You got security clearance."

"What does that mean?"

"Means you ain't gotta be almost strip-searched to see her."

Kelly made a mental note to tonguekiss the hell out of Felix.

She peeled the pass and stuck it to her shirt with shaking hands.

Rita stood from her strained desk chair and reached through the partition to gently touch Kelly's wrist.

Kelly looked at her pretty hazel eyes.

Rita smiled, clearly sensing Kelly's trepidation, and said, "Listen, sweetie. It doesn't really matter what she's like. She won't be able to get to you, not physically anyway. You'll be separated by glass and if you need to get the hell up outta there for any reason, even just to save your own damn sanity, just knock on the door and we'll let you out. You ain't gotta do nothin' you don't wanna do. Okay, sweetie?"

"Thank you." Kelly heaved a relieved sigh. "I'm kind of disappointed I won't get to scratch out her eyes though."

"Sweetie! You *wouldn't* be the first for that!" Rita's laugh rattled the partition window. She pointed to an intimidating, overly-tanned short-haired female guard near a large metal door at the end of the lobby. "That's my girl Doris. Since you got friends in high places, you ain't gotta wait for nothin' *and* you get to take as long as you need. She'll take you to the visitation room. Should only be a few minutes for Fawn to get there. Doris! C'mere!"

Doris stomped to the sign-in counter like a quarterback prepping annihilation. "'Sup, Rita?"

"This here's Kelly. Take her to Room Two for her visitation. I already sent word to have Fawn Schultz brought in."

Doris's eyes spun like pinwheels. "No shit? The Motel Murderess?"

Kelly smiled and relaxed a little. She felt safe and protected beside these two powerhouse women.

"Yep," Kelly said. "And I'm the first, apparently."

"*Girl*! I'm gonna listen outside the door! That bitch ain't never said nothin' to nobody! I wanna hear what the hell she gotta say!"

Eagerly, almost giddy, Doris took Kelly's hand and buzzed them through the rear door, and led the way down a long cinderblocked corridor with office doors and harsh fluorescent lights, through a series of thick metal doors that were opened remotely by guards following their every move via overhead cameras.

After two twists and a few turns into the depth of the prison—Kelly hoped she wouldn't have to flee as she had no clue how many steps they'd made since Rita's desk—they entered a small hallway with numbered doors.

"This here's the quietest visitation wing we got," Doris said. "Just a few rooms for high-profile inmates."

They stopped at a large white metal door numbered 2.

Kelly's stomach lurched and flipped and flopped. "She won't be able to touch me or get to me, right?" she asked for reassurance.

Doris squeezed Kelly's hand. "The room is separated by Plexiglas. She won't be able to touch you. She'll be on the other side with a single guard and you'll be alone on this side."

"And you'll be right outside?"

"Of course. Just knock if you need me or when you're finished."

Doris nodded to the camera above the door. It slowly rolled open.

The room was small, with a camera in each corner, two mismatched metal folding chairs, and a burnt-orange countertop built against thick yellow-tinted floor-to-ceiling Plexiglas. A series of quarter-inch holes were drilled through the glass so visitors and inmates could speak without telephone receivers.

The entire space was lit with blaring white fluorescent lights. Even though Kelly typically rejected fluorescents, she was suddenly so grateful for them. She'd dreaded a dark, damp haunting cellar, like Hannibal Lecter's shithole.

This wasn't that. This looked like the interrogation cells on *L.A. Law* and there was no way Fawn could touch her or spit on her or even get *close* to her from the adjoining room; the countertops and thick glass made sure of that.

Kelly's heartbeat slowed to normal rhythm while Doris gave her shoulder a supportive pinch, then had the door closed behind her.

After it shut and locked, Kelly sat down, crossed her legs . . . and *waited*, in an uncomfortable folding chair, to see the woman who'd murdered her best friend.

Life had a lot of explaining to do.

Kelly wasn't sure what to expect. She hadn't seen pictures of Fawn since her smirking mugshot had been splashed across every newspaper's front page in 1996. She often wondered how or if Fawn had matured. Kelly remembered her as a long-haired, meek, fun-loving girl who'd turned into—or finally exposed herself as—a brutal murderer.

What would she look like now?

What would she *be*?

A born-again Christian secretary?

A badly-permed hairdresser?

A prison gang member making moonshine in her toilet?

Clearly, Kelly had seen too many exploitation prison films.

A siren buzzed.

The door on the other side of the glass opened.

A tall female guard with salt-and-pepper hair who looked like Bea Arthur in *Maude* entered first.

Kelly held her breath.

Maude stepped aside.

And Kelly saw her for the first time in almost ten years.

Fawn.

She shuffled inside, wearing a beige jumpsuit with a dark ponytail and round wire-rimmed glasses, her hands and ankles cuffed and linked together by chains. She jingled like one of Santa's holiday elves.

A bloodthirsty, murdering elf.

When Fawn saw Kelly, she smiled wide and wonderfully bright, her small brown eyes disappearing behind her cheeks, just like the little girl Kelly remembered from pre-teen birthday parties or whenever Berger had cracked a rude joke.

Fawn stood in the doorway and Maude unlocked her shackles. She was shorter than Kelly remembered, and skinnier, but the face was the same, with smooth skin and freckles.

Kelly's heart beat the hell out of her chest.

Fawn sat in the chair opposite Kelly, with nothing but the old countertops and stained Plexiglas separating them.

After almost a decade, and against her own vow to never see this bitch again, Kelly sat face-to-face with Fawn Schultz.

The door shut on Fawn's side with Maude inside the cell, presumably for order or as a witness. Kelly felt safer with her there, just in case Fawn could spontaneously become the Blob and ooze her way through the Plexiglas holes and devour Kelly alive.

"You still wear Gaultier," Fawn said. "I miss perfume."

A chill ran up Kelly's spine.

Fawn could fucking *smell* her.

If she mentioned fava beans and a nice Chianti, Kelly was going to run for her fucking life.

"You look really pretty," Fawn said.

Kelly studied her.

Fawn sat with poker-straight posture, her hands gently folded in her lap; and her voice was still wispy and soft. Even after everything she'd done, Fawn still appeared *delicate*. Kelly couldn't picture this Plain Jane shooting Ford into the dirt, and yet she knew it to be true.

"Aren't you going to ask how I'm doing?" Fawn asked.

Kelly had no intentions of doing that, because she didn't really give a shit. She'd spent a lot of years hoping Fawn was lonely and isolated and silently suffering and, judging by Fawn's boring appearance, Kelly had gotten her wish. But to directly ask how she was doing would not only go against Kelly's instincts, it might give Fawn the wrong impression that Kelly cared.

Because she didn't care, not anymore.

But she still needed this bitch's help.

So Kelly engaged another way, "You've never filed an appeal for reconsideration on the no-parole-ruling."

Fawn giggled. "Why would I? Everyone and your book made sure I'll never get out of here."

She wasn't wrong. The courts and the press and Kelly herself had worked tirelessly to prove the case against Fawn and make sure she never saw freedom again.

"But I'm okay. I got my first degree," Fawn said casually, although Kelly sensed plenty of pride. "Bookkeeping. I'm studying to be a CPA."

Kelly wasn't sure why the hell Fawn wanted to be an accountant since a criminal record—and being incarcerated for *life*—would most likely disqualify her from ever practicing. But if studying kept Fawn occupied and passed the time behind bars, Kelly wouldn't judge it. Kelly didn't know what prison life was like and assumed clinging to a goal, however farfetched, probably brought some kind of comfort.

"You were always good with numbers," Kelly said and regretted it.

Fawn smiled, as if it was the compliment she'd been awaiting.

Kelly didn't want to even *hint* at their shared history—when Fawn had made statistics charts to help Kelly understand their Girl Scout Cookie sales progress in the eighties or when she'd helped Kelly pass algebra classes with long study sessions in the nineties.

"What about you?" Fawn asked eagerly.

"We're not going to do that," Kelly said. "This isn't *The Big Chill*."

"Do what?"

"Reminisce or catch up."

Fawn leaned back in her chair and something shifted. Her joyful smile dropped to a deeply concentrated straight face, as if she'd realized this wasn't the overdue reunion she'd anticipated.

"Well . . ." Fawn folded her arms across her chest and cocked her head. "You obviously didn't come here for a social visit."

"No. I didn't." Kelly couldn't bring herself to fake interest or lie, but she flashed an attempted sincere smile to lessen her sting, something she'd perfected over the years.

"So, let's hear it," Fawn said. "What do you want?"

Kelly had never enjoyed small talk. She was direct and blunt and appreciated the same from others, even murderers, apparently.

"How do you know Grant Carver?" Kelly asked.

Fawn giggled, as if unsurprised by Kelly's question, and suddenly her smile returned, only with a sharp, sinister edge.

"Let me get this straight," she said. "I don't see you for nine and a half years and then you show up out of the fucking blue and expect me to tell you everything you want to know?"

Kelly dug her fingernails into the palms of her hands, out of Fawn's view, to burn off energy.

"This is why I've never contacted you, because of *this*—" Fawn made dramatic, accusatory gestures toward Kelly. "Your selfish, bitchy attitude. You've always been out for yourself, even when we were kids."

Kelly freely admitted she'd been a selfish teenager; it had been all about her a lot of the time. But the moment Fawn had blown up Ford's chest with a single shotgun blast, Kelly had matured ridiculously quick. Murder had a funny way of doing that. Still, having a convicted killer cut her down to size wasn't easy to take.

But Kelly remained calm, fingernailed her palms, and listened. She'd rise above this shit as long as she could.

"You're here because you *want* something," Fawn continued. "Typical Kelly. You *want* me to help you study for the math portion of the SAT. You *want* me to edit your expose for the school paper. You *want* to stay behind and help Frank Overstreet convict your best friends."

Any doubts Kelly might've had about Fawn's potential bitterness were confirmed and she couldn't keep a smile off her face.

"You agreed to see me," Kelly said. "Either you want to help me or you don't, Fawn. Which is it?"

Fawn's next question came fast, like she'd rehearsed it and saved it for this very moment, "Why didn't you interview me for your book?"

Kelly had made a strict, conscious decision to exclude Fawn while researching and writing her bestseller, refusing to seek any information from the Motel Murderess.

"You didn't deserve a voice," Kelly said. "You'd done enough."

"I could've told you a few things," Fawn said defiantly, as if taunting Kelly with possible secrets. "And corrected your mistakes."

Kelly wouldn't bite. "You wouldn't have told me anything, just like you're not telling me anything now."

"Is that so? Well . . . do you think it's a coincidence we ended up at the Fontaine?"

"What do you mean?"

Fawn shrugged playfully.

Kelly rolled her eyes. "*See*? Nothing."

Fawn smiled again. "If I tell you something, will you tell me about Jill and Matty?"

Kelly's insides tightened. She'd protected her friends since childhood and that instinct raged now, defensive to Fawn's inquiry. Jill and Matty would've allowed Kelly to spill a few tidbits to get what she needed, but Kelly wouldn't exercise that freedom. She wouldn't share their hard-earned happiness with a caged killer.

"If you tell me something worth a damn," Kelly said. "I'll consider telling you about *me*, but not them."

Fawn tightened her ponytail and pushed her glasses up her nose and smiled and took her time, as if mulling over Kelly's offer.

Kelly sat patiently, waiting. She refused to negotiate and was ready to stand and leave any second now if Fawn continued the elusive game.

"Grant told us about the Fontaine," Fawn finally said. "He said it was secluded and no one would ever find us there if we laid low."

"I thought Berger just *drove* after you guys left Michigan," Kelly said. "He took backroads and no-name highways to get lost."

"He did, partly. The campsite was random, but the Fontaine wasn't. He had the name and a map from Grant before we left. After we got to the motel, Berger burned the map in the bathtub."

Kelly's chest hurt like she'd been punched.

Just another lie.

The motel—the site of Ford's murder—hadn't been random at all, like Kelly and the FBI and the courts had believed.

Not that it mattered now, nor would it change any outcomes, but hearing she *still* didn't know the full truth to everything hurt. Would it ever end? Would Kelly ever know it all? Probably not.

For now, she'd settle for what she needed to catch Grant.

"How do you even know him?" she asked.

Fawn laughed. "How do you *not* know him, Kelly? He went to our school for two years."

"*What*?"

"He was a junior twice, when we were freshmen and sophomores."

Kelly had been a self-proclaimed selfish bitch in the nineties, focusing on her studies, her fashion, and her close-knit friendship circle. If life didn't directly involve their makeshift Breakfast Club, Kelly hadn't been interested.

Maybe Grant *had* attended Isaac High. Kelly hadn't paid attention to upperclassmen until she was one, but Grant had been a handsome troublemaker. Surely Kelly would've seen him in passing. She could spot a well-worn leather jacket and bad attitude from a mile away.

Then again, she hadn't noticed her best friends Fawn and Berger plotting brutal murders right under her own nose, so Kelly clearly wasn't as observant as she'd always thought.

But Grant being a temporary Isaac High Tiger would explain his connection to Berger and Fawn. They could've met at the cafeteria dumpsters while smoking cigarettes and swapping dark fantasies.

"And *hello*, you don't remember him killing his father?" Fawn asked. "It was in all the papers when we were juniors."

Kelly couldn't recall that either.

What else didn't she remember?

"How did you meet him?" Kelly asked.

"Who cares? Does it matter?"

It didn't. Whether they'd met at the dumpsters or in woodshop or over an adjoining booth at Penis didn't matter, but a few specifics *did*.

"You sent him letters," Kelly said. "Did he send you any?"

Fawn shrugged. "I don't remember."

Kelly wanted to reach through the glass and rip Fawn's hair out by the roots. "How did you know where to mail them?"

"I'm not telling you that."

"You haven't told me anything."

"I don't give shit away for free. If this was a give and take, maybe you'd get something."

Kelly inhaled a deep breath. "What do you want?"

Fawn smiled. "Tell me about Jill and Matty."

"I already told you, *no*."

"Did they go to college? What do they do? Where do they live? Come on, Kelly. Did Matty ever find love again after Ford?"

Hearing Ford's name fall out of Fawn's mouth hit Kelly like a wasp sting. Fawn's tone was casual and giddy, just like the old days when they'd all pile into Berger's rundown Econoline to Dino's Drive-In to see the latest summer releases.

Kelly wasn't sure what kind of tone she'd expected Fawn to have after so many years, probably something like a possessed Regan in *The*

Exorcist, not a teenybopper extra in *Saved by the Bell*. Kelly expected a killer, not her old friend, and certainly not someone who would speak so flippantly about the beautiful young man she'd blasted with a shotgun in an Oklahoma parking lot.

And yet Fawn looked like her old friend, and sounded like her old friend, but she wasn't.

Kelly wouldn't make the mistake of forgetting that.

"I told you, we're not doing that," Kelly said firmly.

Fawn rolled her eyes, almost bored, as if she wanted to play and was annoyed her playmate wasn't interested.

"You told Jill in a letter in ninety-seven there was more to your story," Kelly said. "What did you mean?"

Fawn's shit-eating grin was Joker-worthy. "Have you read my file? It's a thick one. I've read it, like, a hundred times."

Kelly sighed. "Yes, I've read it."

"It's interesting, isn't it? Do you have the *entire* file?"

"I have Overstreet's copy."

"Ooh! That's probably even juicier than the official court copy. Mine doesn't have photos, though. They wouldn't give them to me, said they'd excite me too much. Does your copy have photos, like, of Mason's body?" Fawn's smirk was wicked and made Kelly's skin crawl.

"Yes. The file has photographs. Why?"

Fawn licked her teeth. "You've seen the photos and read the file?"

"*Yes*."

"Even the section on the forensics, like, say fingerprints and the refrigerator door?"

"You mean your murder weapon?"

Fawn flashed a grin, just like she'd flashed the Kookie's Kampsite surveillance camera after brutally attacking the store's cashier in 1996. It had sickened Kelly then, now it just made her angry.

But Kelly heaved a slow sigh, irritated by the elusive cat-and-mouse bullshit but still white-knuckling niceties *just in case*.

"Fawn, I've looked at the pictures and I've read the report," Kelly said. "Every brainiac FBI agent and pathologist and *Encyclopedia-Brown*-wannabe-sleuth has looked at it—"

"Look again."

"Fawn—"

"Look again, Kelly!" Fawn punched the Plexiglas.

Kelly's heart skipped but she didn't flinch. She'd promised herself she wouldn't let Fawn see her sweat—no fears, no tears.

Still, seeing the mousy not-yet-thirty inmate punch protective glass and shout without any warning was unsettling. Kelly's grandmother had always said *unsettling* was the dignified equivalent of *scared fucking shitless.*

Maude—with her hand on her holstered weapon—warned Fawn only once to calm down, and Fawn obliged like a housebroken puppy, reclaiming her composure and folding her hands back into her lap.

Witnessing it pleased Kelly beyond her wildest dreams. Fawn obeyed orders; she was powerless and couldn't actually hurt anyone else. Kelly knew there was nothing left to fear in the once-brutal killer.

Fawn looked directly into Kelly's eyes and said, "Read the file again." Her words were sharp, as if dropping a bombshell breadcrumb.

Maybe she had.

Maybe this was *the* breadcrumb.

Maybe Fawn couldn't—or wouldn't—blatantly reveal the truth and only worked in riddles now and it was up to Kelly to decipher them. Kelly didn't like games—or breadcrumbs due to the carbs—but she made note of this one, because this one seemed important.

"I'll read it again," Kelly agreed.

Fawn sat up straighter. "I know you want answers, Kelly. You want to know why Grant is the way he is or why I am the way I am or why we've done what we've done."

Kelly folded her arms across her chest, waiting.

"You want me to tell you where he is so you can catch him," Fawn added. "But whether or not I've gotten letters from him or if I have his P.O. box address doesn't matter because I don't know where he is."

"You're right," Kelly agreed. "I came here hoping you'd help me find him. I made a mistake."

She slowly pushed back her chair and stood; she's had enough.

She hadn't learned anything, at least nothing substantial, and Fawn's elusive and arrogant games were too much to combat. Kelly's batteries were worn down.

She stepped toward the exit.

But before she knocked for Doris to open it, Fawn asked, "How many times did we watch *Jaws* in Ford's basement with the lights off?"

Kelly turned back to her. "*What?*"

"Fifty? Sixty?" Fawn stood too with a more focused look than she'd had the entire visit. "We had those all-nighters with Berger and Jill and Matty and ate junk food and got scared and laughed at how bad *Jaws: The Revenge* was. God, Ford loved those movies."

Hearing Fawn's crystal-clear memory of their childhood Saturday nights *hurt.* Kelly remembered those nights too—sleepovers with movies rented from Front Row Video, telling ghost stories, eating Jill's mother's mac-n-cheese, and laughing until dawn.

But Kelly was protective of those memories now. She'd shared them with her best friends Jill, Matt and Ford. Fawn and Berger had been there too, but Fawn wasn't allowed to carry the good with her anymore, not after she'd caused the bad.

Besides, Kelly had come for answers, not memories.

Fawn tilted her head and asked, "What did those movies teach us about fishing?"

"What the hell are you talking about?"

Fawn leaned closer to the glass and without a grin or any theatrics, whispered, "If you wanna catch a shark, you need really big bait."

Kelly sucked in a breath and held it.

The proverbial lightbulb flickered over her head.

The turntable needle scratched to a halt.

The wooly curtain rose.

And she knew how to catch Grant Carver.

She fucking *knew*.

Finally.

"I gotta go!" Kelly pounded on the exit door. She couldn't get out of there fast enough.

"Wait!" Fawn said. "One more thing!"

Kelly glanced back to her as Doris opened the door.

"Are Jill and Matty happy?" Fawn asked, as if they were casual girlfriends meeting for brunch, like she hadn't murdered Kelly's best friend and two others. "Are you?"

Kelly didn't want to defuse the momentum jolting through her veins to catch Grant, and yet something in her shifted when she looked at Fawn now. It wasn't pity or forgiveness or gratitude—although Fawn had helped steer her in the right direction—but rather a profound sadness. Kelly had shared a large chunk of her life with this woman and they couldn't be more different—one a murderous criminal, one a successful author—yet Kelly remembered the wannabe prairie girls and Easy-Bake Oven chefs and *My Little Pony* braiders.

But Kelly wouldn't allow memory lane to cloud her judgment.

She pushed in her chair and stood back.

Fawn gave a single nod, as if she understood.

They would never see each other again.

When Kelly sat in the front seat of Felix's '68 Mustang—his prized *Bullitt* replica—she let out a long, deep sigh. She wasn't sure how long she'd been holding her breath.

She cracked the window, letting the cool December air into the warm interior.

Felix squeezed her forearm and asked, "Are you okay?"

His handsome face was concerned, almost scared, as if expecting Kelly to burst into tears or scream or punch the dashboard.

But she didn't.

She smiled instead.

And confidently declared, "I know what to do."

KELLY
8:16 PM PST

On the five-hour drive back to Malibu from the prison, Kelly and Felix formulated a plan, foolproofing and fine-tuning every detail as much as possible, until they were certain it was their best option. Felix made calls for budgetary approval and FBI manpower and technical support, while Kelly wrote notes and called Jill to tell her about Fawn.

But Kelly and Felix's best laid plans had a hitch: convincing two unknowing men—Oliver and Giancarlo—to be their accomplices.

As soon as they entered the Dream House, Kelly and Felix were greeted by them.

"How did it go?" Oliver asked. "Are you okay?"

"I'm fine," Kelly said.

"Your face doesn't look fine. You look like you're trying to solve a Rubik's Cube in the dark. What happened?"

"It was—" Kelly wasn't sure how to put it into words. She wasn't distraught or traumatized, but *energized* for the next step. Give her long pink ears and a drum and she'd be the Energizer Fucking Bunny.

"Kelly? What happened?" Oliver urged.

"Fawn helped, actually," she said. "If you can believe it."

"Well, I might believe it if you told us *how*. Let's hear it!"

Kelly set down her bag, Felix closed the front door, and the house was quiet but for the repetitive waves from the open living room door.

Oliver and Giancarlo looked at each other, clearly confused by Kelly and Felix's reservation.

"Is everything all right?" Giancarlo asked.

"Everything is fine," Felix assured.

"We just, uh—" Kelly still couldn't find a starting point, even though she and Felix had role-played this scenario in the car.

"Just *what*?" Oliver asked. "Spit it out."

Kelly flipped her hair over her shoulders and went for it, "Have you ever seen *Deadliest Catch*? To catch the biggest, deadliest fish, you need really good bait and a really big fucking trap."

"What the hell are you talking about?"

"It was Fawn's idea. Well, sort of. She pointed me in the right direction. I think."

"Are you speaking in tongues now? Kelly!"

Kelly took a breath and refocused, "If we want to catch Grant, we need to use something he can't resist."

"Like what, *me*? That won't work. He thinks I'm dead."

"No . . . not *you*." Kelly's eyes wandered to Giancarlo.

Giancarlo's thick eyebrows creased and he asked, "*Me*?"

"We think Grant wants you dead, but he can't find you. He probably searches the internet for news on himself and Overstreet's death, and probably for your name and Oliver's too." Kelly spoke slowly, carefully, knowing her proposed plan could backfire at any moment once everyone understood it. "Killers are methodical and narcissistic about their own handiwork and their obsessions."

"I don't understand," Giancarlo said.

"Me neither," Oliver said, slightly defensive, as if slowly sniffing out Kelly's plan and not liking the smell.

"What if we put everything Grant's looking for in one place to lure him out of hiding?" Kelly asked. "We throw a fake memorial in Oliver's memory. Plaster it all over the internet with e-vites and a MySpace page and *whatever*. If we invite a shit-ton of people and gain enough exposure, Grant's bound to see it."

"How very hip and Y2K of us," Oliver said. "What does this have to do with Giancarlo?"

Kelly took a breath, looked at Giancarlo, and went for it, "You're the really big bait. You'll be the party's host."

"*What*?" Oliver shrieked. Instinctively, he stepped between Kelly and Giancarlo, even though Giancarlo wasn't in any danger.

Kelly held out her arms to defuse tension. "Hear me out."

"Are you going to call Dateline so they can film this for the next episode of *To Catch a Predator*!" Oliver snapped. "No fucking way! We're not risking Giancarlo's life to catch Grant!"

"Oliver—"

"You want to throw a party for a serial killer? Fuck you, Kelly!"

"Oliver, calm down," Felix said.

"I can't believe you agree with this!" Oliver barked. "The FBI approves of using a civilian to catch a *murderer*?"

"It's not without risks, but we'll pick a location the FBI and LAPD can discreetly protect and apprehend Grant the second he shows his face, before anyone gets hurt."

"Can you guarantee that?"

"There are no guarantees."

Oliver wouldn't let up and breathed fire, "What makes you think he'd even show? Why the hell would he come to some bullshit fake memorial for me anyway?"

Felix didn't respond, Giancarlo remained silent, and they both looked at Kelly.

Oliver turned to Kelly too and asked, "*Well*?"

"Do I really need to answer that?" she asked. "First of all, he won't know it's fake and neither will the attendees because everyone thinks you're dead. Second of all, it's *you*, Oliver. I don't think I need to explain to anyone in this room what you mean to him."

Tears burst through Oliver's forced tough exterior and rolled down his cheeks.

Kelly gently took his hand and softly said, "Yes, he's a murderer and methodical and smart, but he's also in love with you. And I think your death is his one and only regret. You never had a funeral, so he won't be able to miss a memorial in your honor. And if it's thrown by Giancarlo, he might not be able to resist that either—"

"Yeah, to *kill* him!" Oliver jerked away from her touch.

The room fell silent again, none of them sure how to respond.

Then Felix calmly said to Giancarlo, "We wouldn't ask if it wasn't important. You'd be fully protected and at as little risk as possible."

"This is bullshit!" Oliver barked. "There has to be another way!"

"Don't misunderstand, Oliver. I don't *want* to do this," Kelly said firmly. "I don't want Giancarlo or Felix or anyone to risk their lives to catch this homicidal Marlboro Man. I'd rather be sittin' on the dock of the bay watchin' the tide roll away, okay? I don't want any of us to lose anything else, but this is the best chance we've got."

"It's not fair to ask him to do this," Oliver whispered.

"You're right, it's not. And if doesn't want to do it, we'll figure something else out—"

"I'll do it," Giancarlo said, breaking his silence.

They looked at him, his face firm and determined. Kelly and Felix weren't surprised, but Oliver was shocked.

"Giancarlo, no!" He took the beautiful Italian into his arms. "Don't do this! You can't! I won't let you be a pork chop to a panther!"

Giancarlo laughed into the nook of Oliver's neck and whispered, "Óliver, I'll do whatever I can to keep you safe."

Oliver cried and held on tight to Giancarlo's shoulders.

Giancarlo kissed the top of Oliver's head, then looked at Kelly and Felix and asked, "When do you want to do this?"

"Next Sunday," Kelly said.

"That doesn't leave a lot of time, especially this time of year."

"Then we better get started."

"There's one more thing though," Felix said. He stared hard at Oliver and Giancarlo and added, "Once the invitations are sent, everyone will know Giancarlo is in California. It won't be safe for you two to be together, just in case Grant starts tailing Giancarlo."

Oliver immediately held on tighter to Giancarlo, digging his fingers into Giancarlo's shirt, as if the gravity might suddenly give out and he'd float away.

"We have to separate?" Oliver's voice was shaky and scared. "You want to take him away from me after *you* brought him back in the fucking first place?"

"He will be well-protected, Oliver. You both will," Felix said. "It's just a precaution until after the memorial service. We don't want Grant to discover you're alive."

"It's only a week, *amore*," Giancarlo said into Oliver's ear. "I'm not going anywhere."

Oliver hugged him again and whispered into Giancarlo's neck, "This is fucking awful."

Giancarlo squeezed him close, then confidently told Kelly and Felix, "Let's catch this *stronzo*."

"I always did love a good party."

OLIVER MICHAEL FOSTER
August 9, 1976—June 13, 2005

To honor Oliver's remarkable life, a memorial will be held
Sunday, December 18 from 6:30pm to 11pm
at the Roosevelt Hotel in Hollywood

Bring your best stories and pictures of Oliver,
and your appetites, as drinks and
In-N-Out Burger (Oliver's favorite!) will be provided.

Oliver's ashes will be available in a secluded quiet
room for those who wish to pay their respects.

Please RSVP to this email or the MySpace
link below by December 12.

Oliver was the love of my life.
Please join me in saying goodbye.

Con tanto cuore,

Giancarlo Ossani

Oliver Foster Memorial MySpace Link

KELLY

SATURDAY, DECEMBER 10, 2005
11:16 AM PST

Kelly sat at the desk in her bedroom, overlooking the Pacific.

Two framed photographs—one of Jill, Matt and herself at the Hollywood sign during sunset, another with Overstreet wearing Mickey Mouse ears at Disneyland—sat on the desk, watching over her as she reread Fawn's extensive police and FBI files and viewed grisly detailed crime scene photos.

Three soft knocks at the door popped her out of a lazy daze.

Oliver was there and she waved him inside.

"You okay?" he asked, sitting on the edge of her bed.

"Yeah. Just having another look."

They stared at each other and although they hadn't known each other long, they knew each other well. They hadn't really spoken since the heated memorial-discussion the day before, and Giancarlo had left the house shortly after to enter FBI protective custody. And there was now an awkward air between them neither seemed ready to tackle.

But Kelly spoke first, "I'm sorry for asking Giancarlo to do this."

Oliver's shoulders relaxed, as if relieved she'd broken the ice. "I'm sorry I went *Street Fighter* on your ass instead of thinking rationally," he said with a laugh. "It's a good plan. Felix will keep Giancarlo safe."

Kelly smiled and squeezed his kneecap. "How is it, seeing him again? I mean, the way he looks at you—"

"Stop it!" Oliver slapped her hand. "We have a lot of work to do before I can think about how goddamn beautiful his eyes are, okay?"

Kelly stood and kissed his cheek, an unspoken understanding that she wouldn't push the matter any further.

So she switched gears and handed him a chunk of Fawn's file and said, "Get out your fine-tooth comb, Dick Tracy."

Oliver folded his legs and settled in. "What're we looking for?"

"I don't know. The Da Vinci Code? Fawn just said to read her file again, something about fingerprints and the refrigerator."

"Don't you know these files like the back of your hand? Is there really anything you've missed? Maybe she's just Keyser-Söze-ing us?"

"I know this has wild-goose-chase written all over it, but I just want be sure. There was something about the way she said it that makes me think it deserves another look."

"Then let's find it," Oliver said confidently. "My fine-tooth comb is going to be expertly fine-tuned after all this *Mod Squad* shit."

They reread the files—from Fawn's initial arrest record to Berger's detailed blown-off-jaw-bone autopsy report, and the make and model of Fawn's stolen twelve-gauge shotgun to the instant photographs taken with a stolen camera at the Fontaine Motel.

Oliver asked some case-specific questions, but was mostly interested was in Kelly's life pre-Fontaine, before Mason and Berger and Ford were killed, when they'd had a typical nineties teenage life. Kelly was happy to speak of the good ol' days, sharing wacky adventure stories, which in turn led to Oliver sharing his own with Grant and Char. Over those files and crime scene photos, Kelly and Oliver's newfound bond strengthened, cementing a fast friendship they both just *knew* would continue long after fake memorials and caged killers.

When Oliver got further into the forensic photographs, including autopsy pictures of Ford, he held Kelly's hand but didn't speak, as if knowing or fully understanding how difficult the case had not only been for her then, but also reliving it now.

When he saw crime scene photos from Mason Strauss's house, Oliver paid careful attention. He focused on up-close shots of Mason's hands and feet and the refrigerator door handle, but ignored shots of Mason's crushed skull and exposed brains beside the crisper drawer.

"Fawn mentioned the fridge?" he asked.

"Yes." Kelly flipped through folders and files and paper stacks until she had the report on Mason's kitchen. "The refrigerator door, fingerprints, and photos of Mason's body were her only specifics."

Oliver stared at the bloody handle. A few fingerprints were visible through black dusting powder and two imprinted in Mason's blood.

"What does the report say about the door?" he asked.

"There was something irregular about one of the fingerprints," Kelly said, reading from the original report and referencing Overstreet's personal notes. "One of the prints was only a partial because the authorities suspected something unique or deformed about the finger, possibly scarring or partial-fingertip loss."

Oliver stood from the bed and angled a photograph into the sunlight filtering through the open window. He saw a small blue-hued non-blood fleck on the door handle and asked, "What's that?"

Kelly referenced Overstreet's notes again. "A flake of dried paint. I can't read Overstreet's writing on the type, though. *Teach Beau*? *Teach Hive*? Jesus, he had shitty handwriting!"

Oliver dropped the photograph on Kelly's desk and said, "It wasn't scarring or a missing fingertip, it was dried paint on someone's hand blocking the print. Trench Blue Number Five."

Kelly checked the file. Oliver's words matched Overstreet's notes.

"How do you know that?" she asked. "What's Trench Blue?"

"It's a paint color. Grant used it in all of his paintings. He was always covered in it—his fingers, his clothes, his chest hair. I'd find it on my stuff sometimes too—my cheek or my notebooks or the toes of my Chuck Taylors. He left flecks of it everywhere he went. I thought it was the cutest thing—that whole beautiful-tortured-artist *thing*."

Kelly didn't understand.

How had a chip of Grant's favorite paint wound up on the door of Mason Strauss's refrigerator—the scene of Mason's death?

Had Grant been involved?

That didn't fit the official narrative—that Berger and Fawn had returned to Mason's house after attacking him with their friends, brutally killed him, and later made their friends believe they were all collectively responsible—but the uninvestigated paint sample and partial print meant Grant might have been there too . . . and helped killed Mason.

"The paint could be a coincidence," Kelly said.

Oliver adamantly shook his head. "No way. You could only get Trench Blue at one art store in Detroit in ninety-five. We'd drive an hour to pick up tubes of it. I don't know anything about Mason Strauss, but if he was some asshole football jock, I doubt he was buying hard-to-find acrylic paints at some hole-in-the-wall art store."

"But . . . how is that even possible? Mason was killed a year after Grant disappeared. Why would Grant have gone back to Michigan to help Berger and Fawn kill a quarterback?"

"You're asking *me*?" Oliver's pretty Paul Newmans were wide and unknowing. "I fell in love with a guy straight out of *American Psycho*, remember? Clearly, I don't know *shit*." He laughed awkwardly, as if laughing might keep him from crying. "I don't know anything about killers being penpals and I sure as hell don't know anything about them co-sharing or tag-teaming a murder."

Kelly's head hurt.

Had Grant helped kill Mason Strauss?

If this is what Fawn had wanted her to find . . . *why*?

"Look at this," Oliver added, setting another photograph on the desktop. It was a close-up of Mason Strauss's ankles wrapped in duct tape. Oliver pointed to a small edge of the tape, almost out of view of the camera, but showing just enough of a *teeny-tiny* loose flap of tape. It wasn't a tear or a jagged teeth-rip, but *cut*, with crisp straight edges.

Kelly knew getting such a smooth cut on duct tape wasn't easy without scissors. She and Oliver flipped through two more photos of different angles of Mason's ankle.

A third picture—a forensic shot taken after the tape had been removed postmortem—showed the tape had been cut down the middle of the suspicious straight-edge flap.

Kelly held the photo up to the window and curled the edges together, to simulate re-taping the tape, as if still around Mason's ankle.

And there it was: the loose flap reconnected several other flaps . . . and created an intricately-tied bow.

A fucking *bowtie*.

Grant Carver's signature.

The tape had been severed down the middle of the bowtie, which is probably why investigators hadn't caught it before.

Except Overstreet must have.

He'd *known*.

That's why Grant, Fawn and Berger shared an archive box—they'd known each other, been friends, and *killed* together.

And Grant had left his calling card behind on Mason's ankles.

"What is that?" Oliver asked.

"The smoking gun," Kelly whispered. "If that partial fingerprint matches, we've just nailed Grant on another murder."

"*If*. So many *ifs*. Everything about this case is like trying to solve a puzzle on *Wheel of Fortune* with nothing but Z's!" Oliver released a frustrated laugh. "I fucking hate puzzles!"

Kelly gathered her shiny dark hair and tied it into a ponytail. She was tired and overloaded and *confused*. She'd fully believed she'd known the whole story of Fawn and Berger's crimes, of the maniacs who'd killed Ford. But here was more information—more *proof*—that she didn't know it all.

Maybe that had been Fawn's intention, not to point fingers at Grant or to help Kelly find him, but to hold onto power and dangle unknown truths and paper-thin slivers of information to retain control.

"Why would Fawn want you to find this?" Oliver asked again. "I know it rewrites your history, but why would she want you to know if Grant helped her kill Mason?"

Kelly rolled her eyes, finally understanding *why*. "She's bitter I didn't interview her for my book. This is Fawn's way of telling me I'll never know everything, but she will."

"I don't like this bitch."

Kelly laughed.

Oliver laughed too and added, "You're Scooby-Doo and she's that obnoxious, good-for-nothing *Scrappy-Doo*. She sucks."

Kelly laughed harder and louder and it felt good, and she appreciated Oliver knowing she'd needed it.

"Yeah, she sucks," Kelly agreed.

"What's so funny?" Felix asked as he entered the bedroom. He smiled too, the jovial atmosphere clearly contagious.

Kelly pointed to Oliver and said, "*Him*."

Felix kissed Kelly, then sat beside Oliver on the bed. He nodded toward the open files and photos and asked, "Find anything?"

"Yes!" Kelly handed him a photograph of the refrigerator door. "Can you have these prints rerun? There's one unidentified partial on the handle we think is Grant's."

Felix's eyebrows creased. He looked at Oliver, then Kelly, then the photo. "You think Grant helped Berger and Fawn kill Mason Strauss?"

"Yes."

Felix smiled, as if partially surprised, yet impressed by Kelly's keen detective skills. "I'll have them run it against Grant's prints today."

Kelly noticed something in Felix's tone. His patented enthusiasm for uncovering clues dimmed slightly, like something was on his mind.

"Are you okay?" she asked.

"Yeah, it's just—" Felix stopped himself and pulled a small square envelope from his back pocket. It was a shiny DVD in an envelope stamped CONFIDENTIAL in thick black ink.

"What's that?" Oliver asked.

Felix kept his eyes on Kelly and said, "FedEx dropped it off an hour ago. I just watched it. I'll tell you about it, but I won't show you."

Kelly spun in her desk chair to look at him head-on. "Felix, what's going on? What's on it?"

"A video you never want to see it."

"A video of what?"

"You've seen enough already, Kelly."

"Jesus, Felix. What is it, *The Ring*?"

Felix leaned his elbows on his knees and looked directly into Kelly's pretty dark eyes. "Grosse Pointe Police have stitched together surveillance footage of Overstreet on the night he died. ATMs, the post office, a bookstore, and—"

"*And?*"

"It includes his abduction."

Kelly inhaled a slow breath through her nose. She appreciated him protecting her from images of Overstreet's last known moments of life. And he was right—she didn't want to see it, unless absolutely necessary, but she still wanted—*needed*—to know what it showed.

"Tell me what happened," she said.

Felix rubbed his hands over his shaved head, then laced his fingers together. When he spoke, his voice was soft and soothing, just how Kelly liked it, "He was hit on the back of the head in a Trader Joe's parking lot. Cash register receipts and in-store cameras show he'd just purchased a rib eye steak from the meat counter, a bottle of merlot and a slice of carrot cake from the bakery—"

Kelly smiled though teary eyes.

Carrot cake had been Overstreet's favorite; she'd disastrously tried baking him one two years ago for Thanksgiving.

And they'd drunk a lot of merlot together over the years.

Felix continued, "After he was hit, Overstreet struggled and fought back, but the attacker repeatedly hit him with what appears to be a crowbar or a tire iron, just like Jessica said, until he stopped fighting. Overstreet was then put inside the backseat of a white BMW 5 Series and the attacker drove off with him."

Kelly couldn't stop staring at the disc in Felix's hand. She didn't want to watch it; she *couldn't*. Seeing Overstreet's badly-beaten corpse in pictures had broken her heart. She couldn't handle seeing him attacked and kidnapped too.

Her veins hurt from racing red-hot adrenaline. "Was it Grant?"

"The attacker wore a mask." Felix shrugged weakly, like he wanted to have rock-solid answers but didn't. "But the height and shape and strength match. The BMW was reported missing, but it was rented at Metro Airport under the name Billy Fitzgerald."

The room seemed to light up instantaneously, brighter than the Christmas lights Felix had looped around the outside deck banister.

Billy Fitzgerald.

One of Grant's many now-known aliases.

And another nail in his goddamn coffin.

"Airport cameras filmed a man at the Alamo rental desk," Felix added. "It's a grainy image, but it looks like Grant."

Kelly's heart raced.

They were *close*, close to concretely proving Grant had killed Overstreet. She was relieved and motivated, but mostly *vindicated* because her friend's killer wouldn't get away with it.

"So . . ." Oliver gestured to the files and photos and everything they'd learned. "What do we do with all this shit?"

"Give it to the prosecution once Grant is caught," Felix said.

"Okay, but what do we do *now*?"

"We salivate and wait," Kelly said with a wicked grin.

She was confident.

And fucking *ready*.

ONE WEEK LATER

"What's meant to be will always finds a way."
JON IMS

KELLY
SUNDAY, DECEMBER 18, 2005
6:16 PM PST

Just off the front lobby of the hotel, in a separate hallway from the main ballroom, was a small banquet room labeled *The Quiet Room*, with lush carpet and heavy red velvet drapes, quite a contrast to the cheery, colorful lobby and ballroom, which had been transformed into a lively, over-the-top celebration in Oliver's honor. Balloons and photo booths and filled champagne flutes and framed photographs of Oliver stuffed every inch. The air smelled like cotton candy and In-N-Out burgers, all of Oliver's favorite things.

All for a fake wake.

Kelly wasn't sure how the hell Felix and the FBI and their hired party planners had managed to create such a magnificent fake party on such short notice, and during the holidays no less, but here it was, tastefully and respectfully done.

The last week had been difficult, the waiting long and painful, but Kelly and Oliver had spent the time as constructively as they could.

Kelly organized everything she'd discovered on Grant Carver through Overstreet's notes and Oliver's memories and the Michigan storage unit findings; she visited the El Segundo unit, although it provided no leads, just stacks of Grant's paintings (many featuring Oliver's distinctly-recognizable Paul Newmans), jazz records and miscellaneous papers the FBI would investigate; and when she needed a break from murder and clues and investigation, Kelly dipped her toes in the chilly sea water and cuddled with Felix while he talked turbo engines and gear shifts on the cars in the Sean-Connery-only James Bond films.

But Kelly never lost focus or determination to see this through to the end, like she knew Overstreet would expect and appreciate.

Felix followed leads too. The rented BWM used in Overstreet's abduction was found abandoned and torched behind a row of burned-out houses ten miles from the abduction site. Overstreet's blood and the murder weapon were found in the car's scorched backseat—a fingerprint-free crowbar, just like Jessica had predicted.

He also had comparison tests run on the partial fingerprint lifted from Mason Strauss's refrigerator against Grant's prints from his 1995 surrender. The print matched Grant's left middle finger and Felix had the paint chip tested against the paintings found in Grant's El Segundo storage unit too. It matched; Trench Blue Number Five on the fridge door and all fourteen found paintings.

Grant had helped kill Mason Strauss.

Like Kelly, Felix stockpiled all the little things, the small evidentiary proof of Grant's crimes, all to ensure a guilty verdict and stop him for good. It's what they all wanted—to see Grant stopped and jailed and forgotten, not only for themselves, but for Grant's other victims too—the loners and waitresses and hotel managers and everyone he'd killed. Their legacy deserved a proper ending too and Kelly, Felix and Oliver—with Giancarlo's help—were determined to get it for them.

Although Oliver and Giancarlo weren't allowed to see each other during the week for their own protection, Felix gave them untraceable mobile phones so they could at least speak to each other during the separation. They spoke every day, almost constantly, reminiscing and catching up on what they'd been up to since they'd seen each other, while also trying to make sense of Grant Carver's destruction.

But they never spoke about current feelings or the future or what their reunion *meant*. A large proverbial elephant strangled their conversations, loaded with so many unsaid things, but there would be time to explore all that after Grant was caught, after Oliver had his life back, after this was over.

As guests started arriving, Kelly and Felix—who wouldn't leave her side—entered the Quiet Room to double-check everything was in order, although they'd checked and rechecked every inch of the place, from the heavily-armed undercover agents posing as party attendees to the closest exits to Oliver and Giancarlo safely guarded in the hotel's safety deposit vault behind the front desk after smuggling them in via overstuffed laundry carts earlier that afternoon.

Everything was set.

Ready.

The Quiet Room was somber and dark, the overhead lights dimmed in shadowy yellow hues. A large black-and-white portrait of Oliver—taken by Giancarlo on the Amalfi Coast during their Italian summer in 2002—was perched on an easel at the front of the room, beside a flattop podium with a shiny silver urn. Kelly had bought the urn at an antique store in West Hollywood and filled it with Super Scoop cat litter, just in case any grievers—or attending killers—had the morbid curiosity to peek inside.

And while Oliver's favorite sixties and seventies folk-rock played quietly on overhead speakers, Kelly and Felix slowly approached the front of the room, where a tall man with a shaved, almost-bald head and wide shoulders stood facing Oliver's fake ashes.

The memorial hadn't officially started, although guests were arriving through the hotel lobby, but this room hadn't been unveiled yet.

Only someone looking for it would have found it.

Someone who desperately wanted—*needed*—to pay respects to Oliver's ashes.

Someone like Grant Carver.

Could it really be this fucking simple?

Even in low lighting and soft tunes, Kelly's senses were precise.

She just *knew* this tall, broad stranger was the killer she was after.

And he wasn't on time.

He was *early*.

In all the reports she'd read and detailed accounts Oliver had given her, Kelly knew Grant had never been late for anything, always early, like when he'd abandoned Oliver at the Fontaine Motel in the middle of the night—*early*; or when he'd been released from jail after his father's death was declared an act of self-defense and had fled without speaking to anyone—*early*; and now, when he had to be the first one to see Oliver's ashes before anyone else—*early*.

"You just had to be the first," Kelly said softly.

The man turned and faced her, but she didn't immediately recognize him. The only photographs she'd seen of Grant were a decade old, when he'd had long wavy hair and a scruffy beard. This man had a freshly-shaved head nearly to the skin, a clean-shaven face baby-butt-smooth, and paint-stained fingertips.

But the almost-black shark eyes gave him away. Kelly had noticed them in the old pictures and she noticed them now, dark and sinister, the irises blending almost perfectly with the pupils.

But he didn't *look* like the monster she knew he was. He didn't have fangs or horns or crazed eyes or a foaming mouth. He was . . . *handsome* and tall and he smelled good and he wore an expensive black suit with diamond-encrusted cuff links and shiny leather shoes that reflected the dim yellow lights. He looked like a smouldering vintage movie star, like Montgomery Clift or Rock Hudson, not a rabid killer like Charles Manson or the Night Stalker.

His presence was overpowering, commanding and firm.

But Kelly wasn't afraid.

Felix stood beside her with a strong superhero stance with his gun drawn and his sleeve wired with a microphone to a dozen agents following his every move. They'd painstakingly rehearsed strategy. All Felix had to do was say the word and the cavalry would descend with guns blazing.

But the protection didn't make Kelly any braver than she already was. She'd had enough and wanted this to be over. Grant had brutally murdered her dear Overstreet and at least seven others, including Mason Strauss. She refused to back down. She wouldn't show fear or tears, not while Carole King's masterpiece *Tapestry* played overhead, and not in front of an Italian-sunset-lit photograph of Oliver.

Grant grinned, his smile partially crooked, his teeth beautifully white. He put his hands in his trouser pockets and stood with his chest naturally puffed. He was *cool* and handsome and the shaved head suited him. In another circumstance Kelly might've slipped him her number on a cocktail napkin, but knowing who—*what*—he really was made the polished, well-dressed exterior easy to ignore.

"Kelly Spencer," he said with confident recognition, his voice deep and controlled and just loud enough to fill the small space between them, not the entire room. He never looked at Felix, just fixated his dark eyes on Kelly.

She stood still, her arms at her side, and stared back. She'd visited one killer in prison a week ago; she'd face-off with another if she had to, if it won her the endgame.

"Fawn said you were tenacious," Grant said.

With this admission, Grant confirmed he had in fact corresponded with Fawn, that she had told him about Kelly . . . and probably more.

As Kelly's eyes adjusted in to dim light, she could more accurately see little details about Grant she'd missed at first glance. His cufflinks and shoes were streaked with thick dark splashes, and his fingertips weren't paint-stained, they were *wet*.

The weather had been seasonally typical—cool and sunny and postcard-worthy, without a drop a rain, so Kelly knew the shiny splashes on Grant's clothes and hands weren't rainwater.

Somehow, though intuition or studying the idiosyncrasies of this elusive and savage killer, Kelly just *knew* it was something much more sinister: *blood*.

"How did you get in here?" she asked, staring at the dark droplets streaking the freshly-steamed carpet around Grant's shoes.

"Does it matter?" he asked.

Kelly saw a Roosevelt Hotel identification badge clipped to Grant's suit jacket, presumably forged like the storage unit passports. She doubted it was legit, as Grant wouldn't have hidden himself in plain sight as a hotel bellhop or housekeeper.

Again, she somehow knew he'd killed again, that the suspected blood on his hands and body were from a violent entrance, maybe at the hotel's back dock or the underground parking garage. He probably forced and fought and beaten his way inside, because with this murderous motherfucker anything was possible.

Kelly looked at Felix, who was already whispering something into his shirtsleeve microphone. Kelly was confident he'd seen the same suspicious splashes and was ordering another sweep of the building.

Still, Kelly didn't back down and stared at Grant, because he was right about one thing: *how* he'd gotten into the memorial didn't matter. Whether he'd snuck in as a fake employee or worn a bogus glasses-and-moustache combo to look like Groucho Marx or sported a silly mask like the nearby Hollywood Boulevard street performers or used his snake-choking charm to slide past the front doorman or even violently rampaged past a guard or two *didn't matter*.

He was here.

He was caught.

The killing would finally stop.

And yet, Kelly couldn't believe it was so simple.

Felix gave another order, much louder this time, for several agents to clear the party and evacuate the hotel, then called in the bomb squad to search the building just in case Grant had anything besides surrender up his well-dressed but bloodstained sleeves.

Felix stayed with Kelly, his gun drawn, his hands steady.

"You seem surprised," Grant said to Kelly. "Didn't think I'd show?"

"I didn't think you'd make it this easy," she admitted.

A grin slithered across Grant's handsome face. "You don't think I knew this was a setup?"

Kelly wasn't skilled in understanding a killer's motivations or mind games, but she could teach a master class in debunking bullshit. Grant was lying, either to save face or to remain fiercely controlled. He had a little quiver between his thick eyebrows, a lightning-fast flick that showed worry, and it made Kelly smile.

But Grant held strong to the façade and said, "Nice touch with the urn and fake ashes. What is it, kitty litter?" He rubbed his wet fingers together. They were pasty, caked with dust and blood. He'd clearly killed . . . and touched the urn's contents before anyone had arrived.

"Arm & Hammer Super Scoop," Kelly said with little pleasure.

She'd witnessed Ford score countless homeruns in her youth. He'd beamed and peacocked with well-earned pride after every single one. This moment—capturing Grant Carver—was potentially the greatest homerun Kelly might ever score, yet she felt no pride or real satisfaction, because a lot of people had died for this shallow victory, but she was over the goddamn moon Grant couldn't hurt anyone else, and she wanted to hear handcuffs clink around this asshole's wrists.

"I guess this is my surrender," he said. "It must be quite a letdown for you and Dirty Harry here—" Grant nodded toward Felix. "—not being able to surprise me with an arrest. You probably had dramatic movie-worthy takedowns planned, like hogtieing me or blowing my head off or having another spectacular shootout at the Fontaine Motel. Sorry to disappoint you."

Kelly stared at him.

How was this handsome, intelligent, quick-witted man an undercover monster? Kelly had known a lot of charming, successful men, even dated a few. Had they been killers underneath the glossy exteriors too? Berger and Fawn had hidden their thirst for killing and Kelly often doubted her ability to accurately read people, especially strangers.

But she knew for certain Grant was a killer and stopped second-guessing herself.

"I would've liked to have seen you hogtied," she said. "But I appreciate you exposing your weakness and falling for the trap."

Grant's steely stare didn't change or give anything way.

He had one hell of a poker face.

But so did Kelly.

"You claim to know this was a setup, and yet here you are," she said. "Just proves Oliver is your weakness. You couldn't fucking *stand* it, knowing there was a party being thrown in his honor. You *had* to come, just in case it was legit, to pay your respects."

Grant grinned and took a step closer to her.

Felix instinctively raised his gun eye-level, ready to blow Grant's head off in spectacular movie-worthy fashion if necessary.

But Kelly didn't even flinch.

"You're not afraid of me," Grant said. "What if I lash out and make you my last victim before I'm sent to the electric chair?" He smirked, almost playful, as if taunting was all part of the game.

But Kelly wouldn't intimidate easily, not this close to the finish line. "Since Fawn told you who I am, if you wanted me dead, you would've killed me already, long before this party," she said. "And as you can see, Dirty Harry's on point, and he's itching to correct a mistake shaped just like you."

Grant's eyebrows rose approvingly, as if impressed by Kelly's perception, but he confirmed nothing.

"I'm not naïve," Kelly added. "You probably have a gun on you, but I'm sure that feels weird since a gun can't give you the same rush of beating someone to death with your bare hands—like you probably did to whoever stood in your way of getting inside this hotel—because that's what you really get off on, isn't it?"

"You talk too much," Grant said.

Kelly laughed. "Yep, but I have something that'll surprise you."

"I doubt it."

Kelly looked at Felix and nodded.

Felix spoke into his shirt cuff microphone, "Bring him in."

The room's side door, which led to an employees-only hallway, opened. Two very tall male agents entered first. Behind them was Giancarlo, dressed in a black suit and well-worn red Converse sneakers.

Grant's almost-black eyes narrowed, his nostrils flared, and his chest rose and fell with heavy breaths.

Kelly had never witnessed such quick and quiet rage. Her father and Matt's mother had been abusive drunks, but they'd always been boisterous and clumsy before attacking and Fawn had licked her teeth and giggled when she'd killed.

This was different, this was calculated, practiced. Grant controlled his breathing, as if to remain focused, and his body never shook with adrenaline, as if he'd learned to control that too.

Grant reached into his inside suit jacket pocket.

And through the expensive fabric . . .

Against Joni Mitchell's soft soprano . . .

Grant pulled the trigger of a small concealed handgun.

A quick burst of light flashed like a firework.

And the bullet hit Giancarlo's chest.

The beautiful Italian man's body lifted off the ground, slammed into an agent, and hit the floor.

Grant immediately held up his hands in surrender, a wicked grin on his face. Felix kicked the back of Grant's knees and he fell to the floor. Five agents surrounded him and roughly handcuffed him.

Through the shouting agents and clinking cuffs, Grant never lost his satisfied smile.

Until . . .

A voice yelled into the chaos, "Don't hurt him!"

With his face firmly pushed into the floor, Grant looked toward the side door and when he saw the voice's owner, he made a guttural cry, like a wounded animal caught in a bear trap.

In the doorway, surrounded by agents and a now-standing Giancarlo, was Oliver Foster.

"What the fuck!" The carpet muffled Grant's voice. "*Oliver*?" He screamed and struggled for freedom, desperate to stand and get a clear view, his voice deep and grunting, animalistic and desperate.

Two agents lifted him back to his feet, holding his arms tight, while several more kept their guns steadily aimed, ready—*anxious*—for him to make a move.

Grant's mouth hung open like a broken drawbridge. Not only was Giancarlo removing a bulletproof vest, but beside him was the not-dead *Oliver Foster*. Grant could no longer regulate his breathing or keep control. His breaths came quick and sharp and his almost-black eyes filled with tears, like he'd suddenly seen a ghost and was not only shocked and confused, but happy the ghost was actually *alive*.

"*Oliver*," he said again, his voice a delicate whisper. He looked at Kelly, as if she held important answers.

She cracked a satisfied smirk and said, "*Surprise*."

Two paramedics tended to Giancarlo, ensuring he hadn't sustained serious injury from the gunshot. Oliver squeezed his hand just before the medics took him away, then turned to Grant, who was deathgripped inside the agents' hands.

"How? *How*?" Grant cried. "How is this possible?"

Oliver slowly stepped further into the room while the Byrds' *Turn! Turn! Turn!* played overhead. He stopped six feet in front of Grant and studied him, but didn't speak, as if he couldn't find words . . . or wouldn't allow himself to express them.

While staring at Oliver's handsome face and bright Paul Newmans, Grant's knees gave out and he almost dropped to the floor. The agents stood him up, digging their authoritative hands into his biceps.

"Oliver? Are you okay?" Kelly asked.

Oliver's breathing was controlled, his face complacent, neither angry nor sad, but when he looked at Kelly, he flashed a relieved smile.

"Let's go," he told her. He glanced back to Grant and in an almost taunting, ruthless tone added, "I want to be with Giancarlo."

"*Oliver! Oliver*, please!"

Kelly and Felix stepped around the mob arresting Grant and they each took one of Oliver's hands.

The three of them left the Quiet Room.

Not one of them looked back.

OLIVER
MONDAY, DECEMBER 19, 2005
11:06 PM PST

From the Dream House's deck, Oliver watched the waves glisten.

They looked different now, even more beautiful than before.

The colors were different too, more pronounced—the sky electric blue, the beach umbrellas neon pink, the seagulls fluorescent white. Everything was brighter and bolder and prettier than he remembered.

Maybe it was sunnier or warmer than usual.

Or maybe it was *freedom*.

He'd never slept better than the night of Grant's arrest. Nine glorious uninterrupted hours of pure slumber—no night terrors or restlessness or hours spent staring at the ceiling obsessing over every detail of the day, just *peace*. He'd kept the lights on, of course; he didn't expect everything to change at once.

And having beautiful Giancarlo Ossani beside him certainly helped, even though they still hadn't discussed their history or potential future together. But Giancarlo's presence and support only added to Oliver's euphoria. Not even seeing Keanu Reeves's ass in *Point Break* in 1991—which Oliver credited with jumpstarting his sexual awakening—had exhilarated him like this.

But the magic dimmed slightly when Felix and Kelly joined them on the deck, their faces serious and concerned.

"Why do you look like Char's mother after they threatened to cancel *Days of Our Lives*?" Oliver asked, but the joke fell flat.

Felix kept his hands in his pockets and shifted his weight from one foot to the other, obviously nervous and unsure where to start.

"Felix? What's up?"

Felix cleared his throat and said, "Two bureau agents were found in the basement of the hotel, *killed*."

"*What*?" Oliver grasped Giancarlo's hand and held on tight.

"They were guarding a tunnel that links the hotel's basement to a service entrance to the underground parking garage. A dented fire extinguisher was found at the scene with their blood. It was used to bludgeon them to death."

"And you think—" Oliver's voice choked his throat and he coughed to get it out. "It was Grant? That's how he got inside?"

"Yes."

"What did Grant say?"

"He refused to hire an attorney, so the court appointed him one at his arraignment this morning. He now has a public defender fresh out of law school that's in way over her head."

"Why would he refuse a lawyer?"

"We don't know. He's refusing to speak to anyone."

"Can't you, like, *force* him to talk?"

"I'm not RoboCop."

Oliver sensed Felix didn't crack many jokes, but appreciated the pop culture reference, no doubt influenced by Kelly's fascination.

Felix folded his arms across his chest, then put his hands back in his pockets, still nervous of something he hadn't let loose yet.

"Felix, what gives?" Oliver asked.

Felix looked at Kelly, as if the truth would be easier coming from her since she and Oliver had formed a fast friendship.

She nodded and told Oliver, "He won't speak to anyone but you."

Oliver laughed. "Why am I not surprised?"

Grant was a lot of things, although predictable wasn't one of them, but Oliver had expected games to begin the moment he'd been arrested. He'd seen plenty of suspects on *NYPD Blue* desperate to retain bargaining chips or power, fighting until the very last appeal.

"Let me guess, he says he won't give you anything unless he gets a face-to-face with me?"

"Yes," Kelly said.

Oliver looked at Giancarlo, whose handsome smile and sparkling brown eyes made him feel fearless and brave.

"Do I have to see him?" Oliver asked Felix.

"No. You don't," Felix said. "Not if it'll be too hard."

"But do we *need* it? Some kind of confession?"

"We have more than enough to convict him for his crimes, to put him away for the rest of his life or, if the courts decide, to *end* his life."

"*But*?"

Felix took a breath. "We have nothing concrete to prove he killed Frank Overstreet."

Oliver looked at Kelly.

Her chest rose and froze with one sharp breath.

Oliver's neck and ears burned red-hot with an overwhelming responsibility. Not only had he respected and liked Overstreet, he owed the man his life. Overstreet had kept him safe and hidden from danger and been compassionate during the most difficult time of Oliver's life.

But aside from his own personal attachment, Oliver now respected and liked Kelly too. She'd *loved* Overstreet. They'd spent holidays together and worked cases together and she'd inherited his estate. She'd been his goddamn number one. Oliver couldn't let Grant's punishment exclude Overstreet's murder. He'd do whatever he could to help Kelly secure that conviction.

"I'll do it," he said.

Kelly quickly shook her head, as if recognizing Oliver's thought process, and said, "Oliver, *no*. You don't owe me anything. You don't have to face that Ted-Bundy-wannabe for me or anyone else."

"Kelly, are you kidding? Of course I do," Oliver said with a bright smile. "Overstreet deserves his killer Shawshanked. And so do you."

"No, Oliver, you don't have to—"

Oliver held Kelly's hand, just like she'd done to him so many times over the previous weeks. He owed this beautiful woman a lot.

"Grant wouldn't be orange-jumpsuited right now if it wasn't for you," he said. "I was living in fucking *Chattanooga* as some boring guy named Jake Ryan Loeb, feeling sorry for myself, when you blew into town and turned everything upside down."

Oliver's voice broke slightly, but he didn't cry. There was no sadness, just happiness and empowerment and gratitude for Kelly.

"You got me my life back. For Christmas!" he added. "Getting something out of Grant is the least I can do after everything you've done for me. Plus, let's cut the shit here, I probably should see him for myself too, for closure and to say goodbye."

Tears gathered in Kelly's pretty brown eyes, but she too didn't cry or fall into despair. Instead, she hugged Oliver and said, "I know how hard this will be for you."

"I know you know," Oliver whispered.

Kelly kissed his cheek. "You're Scooby-Doo too, *not* Scrappy-Doo."

They broke their embrace, but held hands.

"You just couldn't let me have all the prison visitation fun, could you?" Kelly teased. "I knew you wanted to be Clarice all along!"

Oliver laughed and looked at Felix. "What do you need?"

"Anything about Overstreet," Felix said. "A confession, a *hint*, anything we can use to link him to the murder."

"Anything else?"

"There are a million things, but a big one would be to know where he's been living."

"So you can find out if he had bodies buried under his porch?"

Felix shrugged, defeated. "Yes."

Oliver nodded.

He could do this.

He *would*.

His morning euphoria had been pure bliss. He wanted it every morning. If speaking to Grant Carver was the only way to maintain that high, he'd do whatever necessary.

He looked at Felix and asked, "When?"

"We can go today if you want," Felix said. "This afternoon."

Oliver nodded.

"Whoa! Whoa! *Calmati!*" Giancarlo declared, breaking his silence. He took Oliver's hands away from Kelly's and into his own. "*Amore.* Give yourself some time, a few days at least, *per favore.*"

"There is no rush, Oliver," Felix agreed.

Oliver smiled at Giancarlo, his beautiful olive skin and dark eyes incandescent in the sunlight, and kissed his stubbled cheek.

"I want this to be over," Oliver said. "I want Grant *gone*."

When he'd seen Grant arrested at the hotel, Oliver had begged the agents not to hurt him. It had been an instinctual reaction, from the mouth of the eighteen-year-old lovesick version of himself desperate to protect the charming bad boy he'd met at the cafeteria dumpsters.

But now, in the sparkling December sunshine, among the safety of newfound friends and an old—and possibly new again—lover, Oliver rejected that knee-jerk reaction. He mentally took it back, like it had never happened, because he was done with the past.

Not once in the past eleven years had Oliver ever expected to hear himself say he wanted Grant *gone*, but but he was being honest with himself now, maybe for the first time ever, *finally*.

He wanted to get Grant Carver the fuck out of his life.

For good.

OLIVER
3:16 PM PST

Per Felix's request, Grant Carver was held in the jailhouse before his transfer to a permanent facility in order for Oliver to visit him in a less-severe setting. A private visitation at the jailhouse would eliminate the intimidating experience Kelly had endured visiting Fawn.

But it meant no Plexiglas, only bars separating Oliver from Grant. They could potentially *touch*—which Oliver *for sure* wasn't ready for, and never would be again—but Felix assured Oliver a chair would be placed outside Grant's cell, out of Grant's reach.

Oliver was led down a narrow hallway, past several empty cells, the Alcatraz kind with cinderblocked walls and concrete floors and bunk beds and stainless steel toilet-and-sink combo units.

The hallway and empty cells were eerily quiet. Oliver had always seen rough inmates tongue-wagging and spitting and threatening to kill anyone who'd walked past their cells in the movies, but there was none of that here. He appreciated Felix pulling strings to make this logistically easy as possible—a quiet, private meeting—because emotionally it wouldn't be easy at all.

Oliver had confidently declared to Kelly and Felix and Giancarlo he was ready for this, to see Grant and to get a confession and to wrap everything up with a pretty closure bow, but now that he was here, about to see Grant Carver in person again, he just wanted to puke.

But he'd do it.

He *had* to do it.

He couldn't move on without it.

Felix stopped at the cell at the end of the hall.

Oliver stayed behind him, shaking the nerves out of his hands.

"He's here!" Felix spoke loudly, but didn't shout.

"*Oliver*?"

Hearing Grant's voice speak his name in italics again hurt. Oliver had heard it at the hotel the night before, but this was different. This was going to be just the two of them, like six months ago when Oliver had given up everything to join Grant in California; including almost giving his own life.

Felix looked at Oliver and nodded.

A metal folding chair sat in front of the end cell, several inches beyond the no-reach zone of a thick red paint line running down the center of the hallway.

Oliver took a deep breath, held it, and walked to the end.

Sitting inside the cell on the bottom bunk was Grant Carver, wearing white slippers and an orange jumpsuit, a cigarette tucked behind his ear. Oliver wasn't sure inmates could smoke, but then again, what the hell did he know about jail rules anyway? It didn't really matter since Grant had always broken the rules anyway.

Grant was still handsome, with that James-Dean-Marlon-Brando *coolness* on perfected lockdown, even behind bars.

Oliver hated himself for noticing.

Whenever he'd seen sad, ponytailed women in crime documentaries confessing their love for their violent inmate husbands, Oliver had always wondered how the hell they'd allowed themselves to fall for criminals. But seeing Grant now—orange jumpsuited and beefy— Oliver realized just months ago he was one ponytail away from being the same. He would've burned his life to the ground and looked past all this because of Grant.

But not now, after uncovering the truths to this beautiful monster.

Grant stood from the bed and clutched the cell bars to be as close to Oliver as he could. The collar of his jumpsuit was unbuttoned several inches below his collar bone, exposing a thick patch of dark-blonde chest hair. Oliver couldn't take his eyes off it. He'd combed his fingers through it in his youth, been entranced by it, *turned on* by it, as with Grant's once-shaggy-curled hair. Oliver had clutched handfuls of it when they'd made love. The curls were replaced by a military-grade buzzcut now, but Oliver still *remembered* everything.

And it all confused him, how simple things that had once meant so much and lit a raging fire in his belly and caused rock-hard boners now had no affect on him. Now he felt nothing—nothing for the chest hair or the thick neck or the rough paint-stained fingertips.

But the eyes still had him.

Those damn sparkling almost-black eyes. Oliver had once seen bubbling soda pops and neon dashboard lights sparkle in those eyes, but not now. Now he saw a haunting vacancy he'd never seen before. Maybe it had always been there, but he'd been too smitten, too hypnotized to see the threatening, lifeless glare.

A bright and beautiful smile—the one that had changed Oliver's life in 1994—graced Grant's face as he said, "I didn't think you'd come."

Oliver coughed to get his voice to work and said, "I came."

"I still can't believe it. You're *alive*."

Oliver looked down the hallway at Felix and nodded, letting him know he was okay. Felix nodded back and left.

Although alone with Grant, Oliver was only worried for his heart, not his safety. Felix and a dozen or so other FBI agents and law enforcers were listening to their conversation via mounted cameras and listening devices, and they were only seconds away if Oliver needed help.

Grant held out his hand into the space between them. "*My Oliver.*"

Although he was out of Grant's reach, Oliver still stepped back.

And it wasn't lost on Grant. He retracted his hand and smirked. "You wouldn't have come here if you were afraid of me."

Oliver surprised himself and actually smiled too, because he realized he wasn't afraid. Grant was caged like an animal and couldn't hurt him, not anymore.

"I'm confused," he said. "Not afraid."

"I know." Grant said softly. His eyes wandered briefly, as if searching for something, before returning to Oliver's face. "I saw you jump. I thought you were dead."

"I wanted to be."

"Where have you been?"

"Hiding. From you. The FBI thought you'd come after me if you knew I'd survived. Were they right?"

"*Oliver.*"

"Stop saying my name like that."

"Like what?"

"Like it belongs to you. It doesn't."

Grant never took his eyes off Oliver's Paul Newmans.

"You're refusing to speak to anyone but me?" Oliver asked.

"It's the only way they'd agree to let me see you," Grant said.

"Do you really want to talk or was that just a way to get me here so you could see me again?"

"That depends."

"On what?"

"Is your new partner-in-crime and her Justice League listening to our conversation?"

"You tell me: do the walls have ears?"

"Probably, but I'll tell you anything you want to know anyway."

Oliver chuckled a little. "No, you won't."

Grant slowly gripped the cell bars. "Then why are you here?"

Oliver had lots of reasons: to get a confession for Overstreet's murder, for *all* the murders; to ask why he hadn't been killed too; to ask if everything he'd felt in his youth was real; to tell Grant what an epic *motherfuckingpieceofshit* he was for doing all of this to him and so many others.

But he couldn't vocalize all that, so he said, "Two men were killed at the hotel last night. Is that how you got in, by killing them?"

Grant shrugged. "I have my ways."

"Is that how you escaped your apartment without getting caught after I jumped, with your *ways*?"

"Houdini's got nothing on me."

Oliver took another deep breath.

Getting answers wouldn't be easy.

But nothing with Grant had ever been easy.

Oliver pulled back the metal folding chair a few more inches away from Grant's cell and sat down. Grant in turn sat on the floor of his cell, presumably the closest spot to Oliver he could get.

"Where have you been since I jumped?" Oliver asked.

"Why?" Grant snickered. "Do your Dark Knight detectives think I'm hiding someone in a secret lair?"

"Are you?"

"No."

"Were you trying to find Giancarlo?"

Grant answered quickly, "Yes."

Chills pinpricked their way through Oliver's body, deep-freezing his spine. "Were you going to kill him?"

Grant didn't answer.

He just picked at his bitten fingernails.

Oliver knew it was a confirmation.

He took one more deep breath, until his lungs hurt, and went for it, "Did you kill Frank Overstreet?"

Again, Grant didn't answer, but *smirked*; another nonverbal confirmation, Oliver was certain.

"Why?" Oliver asked. "Why him? Why any of them?"

"*If* I had done any of the things I'm accused of, no explanation would make sense to anybody but me," Grant said casually, without commitment. "And it wouldn't matter anyway."

Oliver agreed. No explanation would justify or even clarify Grant's crimes and Oliver didn't want to hear any more riddles or deflections.

Grant lipped the cigarette from behind his ear and struck a match on the floor to light it, just like he'd done off the Firebird's dashboard or the high school's red bricks. Oliver never knew how the hell he or any movie badasses had managed to do that, but Grant was unique and not much about him was explainable.

Oliver had seen this side of Grant before though, smoking cigarettes to buy time during intense moments. He'd seen it when Grant had confessed his true feelings of love to him in 1994, and when he'd explained killing his father in self-defense in 1995, and again six months ago when he'd confessed he was still deeply in love with Oliver at the Hickory Grove High reunion.

Grant didn't vocally give away anything, but his mannerisms did—blowing smoke rings and picking at his fingernails and avoiding eye contact. He was nervous and struggling to stay in control.

Or he was just methodical—as the murders proved—and the stalling tactics were just part of his process. He'd manipulated and lied and *killed* since the day Oliver had met him, so maybe he was unreadable.

"Do you think I killed Overstreet?" Grant asked.

"It doesn't matter what I *think* because the evidence pretty much proves you killed him, but yes, I do," Oliver said. "I think you blamed him for my death, even though he had nothing to do with it, and you killed him for it. But you've never really needed a reason, have you?"

Grant smirked and smoked. "You've always had such a beautiful imagination. I've always loved that about you."

Oliver deflected the distractive flattery with a fake smile and kept chasing answers, "What I can't imagine is why you didn't kill me too."

Smoke billowed from Grant's nose like a dragon. "I would never hurt you."

"What makes me any different?"

Grant's head tilted and his expression softened. "You're the love of my life, *Oliver*. My first and my only. It will always be you, *only* you."

Despite everything, Oliver believed him. He could see it in those damn almost-black eyes: Grant still loved him and it was real.

Oliver wanted to remember the 1994-version of Grant, the loving, handsome troublemaker he'd immortalized for a decade, but he couldn't see anything beyond the iron bars and the orange jumpsuit and the way his *beautiful imagination* helped him mentally visualize Grant brutally beating his victims to death.

Suddenly, something shifted in Oliver.

He didn't love this troublemaker anymore.

He felt nothing, just *numb*.

He'd almost ended his life for this monster, *twice*.

He wouldn't give anymore of himself.

"Will I ever see you again?" Grant asked.

Damn.

Oliver hadn't thought of that.

He fucking hoped not.

He wanted to move on, to get a goddamn life and put all this behind him, but the smarter part of his brain overruled his emotions and said, "Probably, if there's a trial."

"*If?*" Grant scoffed. "Of course there'll be a trial."

"You killed a lot of people in states with the death penalty. They're going to kill you for what you've done."

Grant squashed his cigarette on the floor, more stalling.

"If they're recording the conversation," Oliver added. "They might use it against you in court."

"I'll say I made it all up."

"Did you?"

Grant grinned again. "What do you think?"

"If you confess, you could make a deal to save your own life."

"You want me to live?"

Oliver hadn't thought of that either, not in depth anyway, and considering it now surprisingly had no affect on him. He didn't feel sadness or shame or fear of never seeing Grant again or in thinking of Grant dead. It just felt stagnant, like the necessary end he was after.

But he couldn't bring himself to voice his indifference and instead said, "It's not up to me."

Grant laughed awkwardly, as if he'd hoped for a different answer, and said, "I'm a fighter. I'll go down swinging before I ever give up."

"Well, I guess that's it then. If you're not going to tell me anything, I shouldn't be here." Oliver stood and Grant quickly jumped to his feet.

"Don't go!" Grant said with more urgency than he'd probably intended. "Stay, please. Just a little longer."

"On our first date, you said you'd let me down eventually because it's what you do," Oliver recalled. "I guess you kept your word."

"*Oliver!*"

Oliver glanced to the end of the hall. Felix was there and nodded.

"See ya," Oliver called over his shoulder and headed toward Felix.

"Wait! *Oliver!*"

Oliver kept walking.

"*Oliver!* Please! *Please!*" Grant's voice was thunderous, like when he'd broke into the bedroom Oliver had barricaded himself in before jumping off the balcony. He'd been sinister and threatening then, but this was different. This was *desperate.* "I'll tell you whatever you want!"

Still, Oliver walked.

"I'll tell you about El Segundo!" Grant shouted.

Oliver stopped and *slowly* turned back, his curiosity too strong.

Knowing Grant was probably just dangling a no-real-info carrot in an attempt to spend more time with him didn't stop Oliver from walking back to Grant's cell. He stood near the folding chair, his toes just over the thick red line. He wasn't afraid. Even if Grant could reach him, Oliver didn't think he would.

Grant stared at Oliver's waiting face and asked, "Your *Columbo* sidekick found my storage unit in El Segundo?"

"Yes," Oliver answered.

Grant pressed his face against the bars and whispered, "It has two hanging fluorescent lights. Behind the rear light is a small panel screwed into the ceiling. It looks like part of the electrics, so the feds wouldn't have checked it. Behind the panel is a small storage space."

Oliver's heart thumped. "What's in it?"

"Everything you want to know."

"Just tell me."

"Don't make me say it."

Oliver sighed. "You have to say *something*—"

"Oh, there's plenty I can say, *Oliver*." Grant spoke quickly, as if afraid of their expiring time. "But let me start with this: no matter what happens—if you uncover all my truths or you forget me or I die in here—nothing will ever change the way I feel about you."

Oliver saw his own reflection in Grant's eyes, just like the first time they'd met behind the cafeteria in 1994. He hadn't seen that in anyone else, not even Giancarlo, and it reminded Oliver how special and important he'd felt as a teenager with Grant.

"But the most important thing you need to know is this: nothing I've done was because of you. Nothing was your fault, you didn't cause me to do anything, and I've never had anything but love for you."

Again, Oliver believed him, but it didn't matter, not anymore.

Oliver would hold on to their first kiss in the Firebird and sharing popcorn at Dino's Drive-In and making love underneath the stars, and he'd be grateful those experiences had helped shape him, but everything else would be forgotten—the Fontaine Motel abandonment, the killings, the attempts to take his own life. Outside of being a potential witness for the prosecution, Oliver never intended to see Grant again.

The serenity of that realization calmed his racing heart.

"I'm going to go now," Oliver said quietly.

Grant stared at him and nodded once, quickly, as if he understood and was giving Oliver permission to leave.

Again, Oliver saw his own reflection in Grant's eyes, where the soda pops from had once danced, then walked away.

Grant didn't call out or beg him to stop.

And Oliver didn't rush or run or feel any real need to escape. He took his time, walking at a normal pace, and he did not look back.

Once he reached the end of the hall, Felix asked, "Are you okay?"

Oliver nodded and they left the hallway. On the other side of a large steel door was Kelly, holding a freshly-glazed donut and an ice-cold can of Dr. Pepper.

"Eat this!" she ordered. "You fucking earned it!"

Oliver laughed and it bounced off the cinderblocks, but it quickly turned to tears. He hugged Kelly and released heavy cries on her shoulder. He wasn't upset or scared or hurt, just *relieved*.

And he ate that fucking donut like it owed him money.

And guzzled Dr. Pepper.

And slowly started to feel like himself again.

"Are you okay?" Kelly asked.

He nodded and released a long, deep breath; he wasn't sure how long he'd been holding it, months probably.

"I'm sorry I couldn't get anything out of him," he told Felix.

"You're wrong, Oliver," Felix said. "We got everything we need."

Oliver ping-ponged between their faces. "What do you mean?"

"I just got off the phone with the agents at the El Segundo storage unit. They're reprocessing the scene since Grant's arrest yesterday and they checked the ceiling panel that Grant mentioned."

"That was fast. *And*?"

Felix looked to Kelly, as if handing her the baton.

"They found five wallets belonging to four men and one woman," she said. "The FBI's checking now, but a few have been confirmed as dead, *killed*, with duct tape bow tie restraints."

"You got all of that within the last few minutes?" Oliver asked.

Felix grinned. "We're the FBI."

"So . . . you mean—" Oliver swallowed hard.

"Grant wasn't dormant for the ten years between his known kills," Kelly continued. "These new murders were in small towns, scattered across the country. Local law enforcement hadn't contacted the FBI because they'd assumed they were freakish one-off killings that didn't warrant larger investigations, that's why they weren't in any databases when Grant's methods were searched."

Oliver hadn't given much thought to Grant's possible dormancy—or lack thereof—since it was too scary to think he'd been killing nonstop from state-to-state for a decade.

And although he felt pain for the victims on an ever-growing kill list, Oliver still sensed there was something Kelly hadn't yet revealed.

"What aren't you telling me?" he asked her.

"One of the wallets they found was Overstreet's," she whispered.

Oliver's heart skipped two beats, then two more. He couldn't believe it and needed clarification, "You mean—"

"Grant giving you the hidden panel was a confession, Oliver."

"Is it enough?"

"Yes," Felix said. "He'll be charged with Overstreet's murder."

"It's over," Kelly said, her eyes now wet with happy tears.

A chill tingled Oliver's fingertips and toes.

Suddenly—*instantaneously*—he had his life back.

No more witness protection.

No more Chattanooga or Jake Ryan Loeb.

He was *free*.

He didn't think he'd find freedom in a place with metal bars and bulletproof glass and armed guards and no natural air flow, but here it was, sweeping over him in a stuffy cinderblocked hallway, swirling between him and two wonderful people he hadn't known two weeks ago but now couldn't imagine life without.

Kelly laughed, as if she too shared the same sudden euphoria.

They cried and squeezed each other close.

And Felix hugged them both.

They'd wanted to catch Grant and get Oliver his life back.

And here it was.

Finished.

Caught.

Freedom.

Life.

KELLY

When Kelly opened her front door after the bell rang, she saw Char, her violet eyes sparkling in the bright California sunshine. They smiled at each other and Kelly noticed she seemed relaxed for the first time since they'd met, and probably long before that.

"What are you doing here?" Kelly asked. She barely knew Char and they didn't share a friendship, but Char had helped Kelly a lot and seeing her was a welcomed surprise.

"Oliver told me it's safe to see him now because that murderous motherfucker is finally caught!" Char threw up her hands with a cheer. In each hand she held expensive bottles of champagne. "So I caught a flight out of the frozen tundra to see him!"

Kelly peeked over her shoulder but didn't see anyone else. "He's no here. He isn't with you?"

"He's at some bar with Giancarlo. The Crab Trap or the Crab's Crotch or *something*. I don't remember what it's called."

Kelly laughed. "The Crabby Cabana. It's Nate's bar."

Char rolled her eyes. "California is crazy as hell. I'm meeting him there in a minute. I wanted to talk to you alone first, if that's all right."

"Of course. Come in."

Kelly stepped aside and Char entered the beautiful, bright home.

"Holy shit! Look at this house!" Char set the booze on the dining room table. "I need to write a best-selling book and move to the fucking beach too!"

Kelly laughed again.

Char was different this time—loose, free, foulmouthed. *Herself.* Kelly liked this version much better than the resistant, arrogant bitch she'd met on the icy Denver streets two weeks earlier.

"Are you thirsty?" Kelly asked.

"No. I'm still a little tipsy from too much wine on the plane."

Char wandered the kitchen and dining room, looking at framed photographs and a shelf of vintage cookbooks, and avoided Kelly's face, as if unsure of what to say or how to say it.

"Are you okay?" Kelly asked.

Char flipped her hair and her eyes finally focused on Kelly's face. "I've spent my life with Oliver in a very *Will and Grace* relationship," she said. "I took care of him and focused on work and the truth is I don't really have any other friends. I never made any, just Oliver. And I *for sure* never made a connection with another woman. All the women I've met have wanted to grab me by the hair and yank me into a pool like a scene from *Melrose Place*."

"What's your point, Char?"

"I know you and I don't really know each other and I promise this isn't a *Single White Female* situation, but maybe we could be friends?"

Kelly smiled, assuming Oliver had told Char about everything they'd discovered and been through to capture Grant, and about their newly-sparked friendship. Kelly was touched that Char wanted inclusion. Love and friendship was the least Kelly could give as gratitude for everything Oliver and Char had done to help catch Overstreet's killer.

Plus, Kelly really liked them both.

Even Char.

The bitch.

"When do you leave?" Kelly asked.

"Day after tomorrow," Char said.

"Nope." Kelly shook her head. "Everyone spends Christmas and New Years at my place. You and Oliver and Giancarlo can stay too. Your *Vogue*-wannabe magazine can wait a week or two for its *head-bitch-in-charge* to return."

Char smiled, awkwardly at first, as if she wasn't sure what to do with such an invite. Then her face softened and she genuinely grinned, like when the Grinch's heart grew three sizes.

"You sure?" she asked.

"Yes. There's plenty of room. Besides, we're all family now. That's Overstreet's last gift to us."

Kelly pulled Char into a hug. Char's hair smelled like citrus fruit, just like Jill's had the first time Kelly had seen her after the Fontaine Motel shooting. Kelly wasn't sure why she remembered that, or even made the comparison now. Maybe citrus fruit was a more pleasant memory than the pain surrounding everything else, or maybe Kelly had found and surrounded herself with like-minded shampoo-positive women. Whatever the reason, Kelly squeezed Char close and Char eagerly squeezed back.

"And after the holidays," Kelly added. "Go home and call me."

"Why?"

"Because that's what friends do, bitch. They call each other."

Char laughed until it faded and her awkwardness returned. She pointed to the champagne on the dining room table and said, "Booze is my olive branch, my way of saying thank you for . . . *everything*."

"You're welcome. And thank *you*. You made a pretty good informant, but Oliver made a much better Cagney to my Lacey."

Char smiled again softly, as if touched by Kelly's sentiment, then checked her watch as if to avoid any further emotion. "I'm going to the Crab Shack . . . or the Crab Club . . . or . . . Fuck! What's it called?"

"The Crabby Cabana."

Char rolled her eyes again. "You want to come?"

"I'll be right behind you."

A car door shut outside the house. They glanced out the kitchen window and saw Felix on the phone beside his vintage '68 Mustang.

"Mm mm mm," Char groaned approvingly. "Who the hell is *that*?"

Kelly laughed. "My boyfriend, Felix."

"Please tell me he drives that car for all the right reasons."

"Yep! He's always wanted to be Steve McQueen."

"Hot damn!" Char cheered. "Anyway, I've always known how to read my cue cards, so I'll leave you two alone. Meet us at the bar."

Kelly walked Char to the door just as Felix reached it.

"Hey, Bullitt!" Char said to him and left.

Kelly laughed and gave Felix a quick *hello* kiss.

Felix closed his phone and asked, "Who was that?"

"Char." Kelly waved to her as she drove off, then held Felix's hand and led him inside. "She's meeting Oliver and Giancarlo at the Cabana if we want to join them."

"That sounds good," Felix said. "But I have news first."

They sat in the living room near the lit Christmas tree while Johnny Mathis's *Sounds of Christmas* album spun on the turntable. The Dream House was cozy and warm and full of life again. And under the tree was Kelly's golden envelope to Overstreet, his seasonal pass to his favorite golf course. He'd never open it and she'd eventually return or regift it, but for now it would sit under the tree as a festive reminder to the love she had for her friend.

Felix held Kelly's hand and said, "The Director wants to meet you."

"A director? You know I won't sell my book to Hollywood—"

"No, the Director of the FBI."

Kelly laughed. "Like my *Clueless* nineties' muse Cher Horowitz always said, '*As if!*'"

"I'm serious, Kelly." And he was—the creased lines between his eyebrows proved that—but they didn't actually explain anything.

"Doesn't he have bigger fish to fry?" she asked. "Like, shouldn't he revisit the Zodiac case or find the Oakland County Child Killer instead of having afternoon tea with me?"

"He's impressed."

"Why? With what?"

"Kill the modesty, Kelly. You brought your friend's killer to justice in three weeks. The FBI and local police—*professionals*— were on the case for ten *years* and couldn't solve it."

"What can I say? I'm an impatient Jessica Fletcher."

"Yeah, and the Director wants to acknowledge that. It's an honor. He doesn't meet civilians often and he's invited us to his home in D.C."

Kelly had never been interested in praise. When her book had been released, her publishers and agent had pushed for her to do the late-night talk show circuit and magazine covers. She'd passed, wanting her book and her anti-violence message to speak for themselves.

When the book became an overnight sensation without any self-promotion, the press became even more feverish. Kelly eventually gave a few press and TV interviews, but after the true-crime writing awards and the hefty paychecks rolled in, she traded all that potential notoriety and celebrity for a quiet life at the beach.

And although she almost always passed on meetings with powerful people too, she wouldn't turn her nose up at the Director of the FBI. Overstreet had respected him; that was worth returning, and Felix was practically giddy over the idea.

"I'll meet him," Kelly agreed. "*After* the funeral and the holidays."

Felix smiled—*beamed*—and said, "I know you once said you didn't have another book in you, but maybe all this is your next story to tell."

Kelly tried to flash a nonchalant grin, but Felix didn't buy it.

"You already started, didn't you?" he asked.

Kelly laughed. How the hell could he read her so well?

And yeah, she'd taken ridiculously large amounts of notes since the day she'd identified Overstreet's body, but another book? A follow-up? After her last, Kelly's publishers had pressured her to write a quickie cash-in to capitalize on the large newfound fanbase, even spoon-feeding a few true crime suggestions, but she'd passed.

And now, Oliver and Grant's story wasn't necessarily hers to tell, although she was in the thick of it. She knew Oliver would give his blessing and Grant didn't get a say.

So . . . *maybe* she had another book in her; one more to finish a story that started before but didn't end at the Fontaine Motel.

"We'll see," she told Felix, which was pure confirmation.

He kissed her cheek and said, "You're incredible."

"Are you going to gush now and tell me you're proud of me?"

"Of course, but it's more than that." Felix remained focused on her pretty face. "I'm proud to be *with* you. I'm proud that you picked me."

Kelly's smile dropped. Felix had always treated her well and spoiled her on birthdays and Christmases with lavish gifts and vacations and home-cooked meals—caring, physical things he could do or give to show his love. But he'd never been vocally romantic or able to express himself through words. Hearing it now set Kelly off kilter, surprised, yet with all the warm-n-fuzzies her fifth grade teacher Mrs. Fitz had told her about.

And Felix kept going, "My father always took my mother for granted. He just expected too much from her—cooking and cleaning and being the perfect housewife with no life or identity of her own. His life defined hers. He was a real piece of shit and he was never proud of her." He held Kelly's face in his large hands. "So, to clarify, just so you'll never have any doubts, I want to tell you now: I'm proud of you. If my life is defined by yours, I'll be a really lucky sonofabitch."

Kelly held her breath. She'd only heard this kind of romance in the trashy novels her mother kept on the back of her toilet. But they were real now, in person, and directed at *her*, from the man she loved more than any other *sonofabitch* she'd ever met.

Overstreet had set her up well. He'd known Felix was the right guy for her from the start. And just like everything else, he'd been right. He'd had a knack for that.

Kelly suddenly realized being happy was all Overstreet had ever wanted for her and she owed this happiness to him. She owed him a lot, and being *happy* was the best way to honor him.

Kelly gently touched Felix's face too and kissed him. She wanted them to remember this moment, when they'd both wholeheartedly and finally acknowledged the love between them. Even though Felix had that macho-law-enforcement-bravado *thing* going on, she knew this was his way of telling her so.

Still, Kelly wanted to be clear, so she hugged him close and delicately whispered in his ear, "I love you too."

KELLY & OLIVER
WEDNESDAY, DECEMBER 21, 2005
3:37 PM PST

The sun was high and bright in the big blue Malibu sky, reflecting off the ocean and warming the cool sand. Jill, Nate and Char sat on a vintage *Beverly Hills, 90210* beach towel watching Giancarlo play in the water with Little Ford, while Matt and Casey built a sandcastle nearby. Surfers caught waves and seagulls caught French fries and the air was filled with laughter and *life*—an idyllic, picturesque coastal afternoon.

Kelly and Felix joined their friends after a morning meeting, arriving with a cooler of iced beer and freshly-made vegetarian sandwiches. Kelly saw Oliver standing ankle-deep in the ocean, away from everyone else on his own, arms folded, looking out to sparkling water. He looked contemplative, as if searching the sea for answers.

She took off her shoes and stepped closer to him. Oliver's face was wet with tears but he wasn't crying. She'd seen this face before, in her friends and herself, with relieved, happy tears.

She nudged his left shoulder with her right.

He smiled and nudged her back.

"My grandmother always said, 'If it doesn't end in tears, it didn't matter," Kelly said, her voice soft and wispy over the waves. "It's the end of this part of our lives. And a lot of it mattered."

"It feels—" Oliver searched for the right word. "*Funny.*"

"Being free?"

Oliver laughed a little, baffled, as if she'd read his mind. "*Yeah.* Not having to wonder or worry or fear him anymore. I don't know how to explain it. I've lived with it—with *him*, in one way or another—for so long. Ten years. I don't remember a time in my life when he wasn't part of it and now I don't know how else to be or who I am without him. I mean, what the hell do I do now? What's the purpose of my life?"

Kelly closed her eyes and stared toward the sun. She'd been living in Los Angeles for nearly a decade and still couldn't believe how sunny and beautiful the winters were.

"Remember the night we drove to Detroit?" she asked. "I told you how I had to grieve Ford and everything else I lost with him?"

"Yeah."

"You need to grieve Grant. Even though he's not dead, you need to grieve him and your feelings and your old life."

"You make it sound so easy."

"It's not."

"How did you do it?"

"Overstreet told me to give myself a year, that after a year I'd start to feel like myself again. And he was right."

"A *year*?" Oliver choked on the word.

Kelly could see fear in his eyes, that same hopeless desperation she'd had during an impossibly long year of holidays and seasons and life without Ford. A year was long and really fucking scary.

But Kelly smiled and said, "After everything you went through six months ago, it'll be a breeze. You won't believe how different you'll feel, how different you'll *be*. I didn't believe it either, but it's true."

Oliver grinned, like maybe he believed her, like maybe her optimism was authentic and just within his reach. He held her hand and said, "I don't know how to thank you for what you've done."

"Stop. If we're dishing out thank yous, let me go first." Kelly's beautiful white smile sparkled in the sunlight. "I know the confession you got out of Grant will just add to the long grocery list of his crimes and convictions, but it means so much to me that he'll be punished for Overstreet's death. Thank you for helping me catch that Mickey-Knox-*Natural-Born-Killers*-wannabe bastard."

Oliver shared her smile. "You did most of the work *and* you got me my life back. How I can ever repay you?"

Kelly glanced at her friends, eating sandwiches and drinking beer, laughing and *living*. Overstreet had brought Kelly and Oliver together, and they in turn brought this group of people together, creating an unconventional family, everyone with nothing but love to share.

There was nothing to repay; happiness was the repayment.

Giancarlo looked at Kelly and Oliver as Little Ford tossed seaweed over his shoulders. Giancarlo's smile was beaming and beautiful.

They waved back, then Kelly leaned closer to Oliver and said, "He looks at you like you're a brand new box of Pop-Tarts and he's *hungry*."

Oliver giggled. Kelly wasn't wrong. Giancarlo looked at him longingly, lovingly, *hungrily*.

"Be happy, Oliver," Kelly added. "That's how you thank me. That's how I thank Ford and how I'll thank Overstreet, by being *happy*."

Oliver studied the handsome Italian man and he suddenly felt more awake and alive than ever before, even more than the first day he'd met Grant. Seeing Giancarlo now, magnificently backlit by California sunshine and flashing his impossibly wide smile, Oliver knew with absolute certainty he was in love with him, that he always had been, and that the life he'd dreamed of was right in front of him, splashing in the Pacific, waiting patiently to make him happy.

And Oliver knew it wasn't sentimental attachment or transferred relief after surviving the Grant manhunt. It was real. It always had been, and with his toes in the wet sand and his eyes on Giancarlo's beautiful face, Oliver knew he was on the brink of something wonderful, of *everything*. All he had to do was jump, this time for *life*.

He looked back to Kelly. She smiled, as if she knew—just like she'd known everything else—that he was finally *awake*. And he was happy to share this moment with a new friend who now felt lifelong.

"Tell him, *everything*," Kelly urged. "Like my grandmother always said, 'Listen to your heart. It might be on the left, but it's always right.'"

Oliver hugged her. She smelled like peppermint and the air smelled like change. He felt warm and gooey and understood.

They walked over to Giancarlo and Kelly scooped Little Ford out of the sea and spun him around. The toddler giggled and twirled his little fingers through Kelly's hair.

Giancarlo stood in the shallow water, his wet blue jeans rolled up his legs, his dark eyes sparkling in the sunlight. He stared at Oliver and splashed seawater on Oliver's calves.

"That li'l bambino is *bellissimo*," Giancarlo declared.

"He is," Oliver agreed.

"Are you okay, Óliver?"

Oliver held out his hand and wiggled his fingers. "Can we talk?"

Giancarlo took Oliver's hand. "What is it, *amore*?"

Oliver nodded toward the pier. "Let's walk."

They lazily walked in the shallows, gently swinging their linked hands between them.

"I'm happy you're here," Oliver said quietly.

The beach was rowdy, but Giancarlo heard him clearly and he smiled, like Oliver had declared it over a loudspeaker or telepathically.

"I'm happy too, Óliver. I want to be where ever you are."

Oliver took a breath and went for it, "Always?"

Giancarlo stopped walking and focused on Oliver's face.

Oliver's heart raced. "Do you want to be where I am *always*?"

Giancarlo blushed and whispered, "*Sì*."

Oliver kissed Giancarlo's knuckles, then his mouth.

The kiss was warm and wet, simple and soft.

And wonderful.

Oliver once believed his first kiss with Grant Carver had been the benchmark for his life, that every kiss he'd ever have would be measured against it. But now, as he kissed Giancarlo Ossani with their bare feet in the Malibu shore, he realized his life was peppered with a variety of benchmarks that had shaped and defined him. That first kiss in Grant's Firebird in 1994 had been magical and had set his life on fire, but Oliver felt that fire again now, only with a fierce, scorching heat he couldn't remember from his youth.

This was pure magic.

Maybe that first kiss with Grant wasn't a benchmark at all, but a bookmark, a temporary holding place in his heart to reference until he'd finished his story. Now he felt like he'd reached the ending, the one he'd needed and wanted and deserved.

He *deserved* this.

He knew that now, not just for himself, but for Giancarlo too, who'd loved with him for years, through everything, *beyond* through.

Oliver wanted to tell Giancarlo what was happening inside him— the lightning bolts ping-ponging through his veins, the swelling heart, the realization of love. But he needed to be clear and honest first.

So he took a deep breath and said, "When we were together—"

But Giancarlo quickly interrupted, "You don't have to do this."

"Yes, I do. Please let me."

Giancarlo nodded once, an unspoken permission slip.

Oliver continued, "You made me happy. I was just too hung up on the past to realize it or appreciate it. You were so wonderful to me. I didn't deserve it. I'm sorry I hurt you."

Giancarlo sucked in a breath and held it, like he'd needed to hear those words and that everything had been worth it and finally made sense, and said, "You did deserve it. You still do."

Oliver felt incandescent, shining brighter than the sunshine. "I want to live by the water."

Giancarlo laughed. "*Che cosa?*"

"From now on, I want to live by the ocean."

The last thing Oliver had seen when he'd jumped from Grant's apartment was the big, blue, never-ending Pacific. He'd hoped it might save him, as if calling him, giving him the courage to jump to save himself. He wanted to hold onto that feeling, the safety he felt beside the water. He felt alive here, with his friends and this beautiful Italian man.

"Whatever you want, *amore*," Giancarlo said. "We can stay here or go back to Vancouver or I'll take you back to Italy. We were happy there. Papà will be so happy to see you again." He blushed and smiled awkwardly, as if he couldn't believe this conversation was real.

Oliver smiled too and imagined waking up beside Giancarlo in that same high-ceilinged flat they'd shared on the Tyrrhenian Sea in 2002, soft summer breezes gliding over their sun-kissed bodies.

Oliver laughed.

Recapturing that once real-life fantasy seemed so silly and surreal.

And yet . . . *possible*.

After wasting so many years and tears of his life on Grant, Oliver wasn't sure what to do with *possibility*, with a real future, with someone else, with *love*, but he wanted to find out.

"If we go back to Positano—" A devilish grin graced Oliver's handsome face. "And live by the water, will you let me have my turn?"

"*Il tuo turno*?"

"Will you let me make you happy? It's my turn."

Giancarlo's smile morphed from awkward to pure bliss. "*Sì! Sì, amore*." He took Oliver in his arms and ran his fingers through Oliver's hair, leaving his hand on the back of Oliver's neck. "When the sun rises tomorrow, we'll start again."

Oliver believed him.

And Oliver was ready.

Ready for Giancarlo.

Ready for life.

And ready for love.

True love.

Finally.

Later that night, after passionately making up for lost time, and for the first time in a decade, Oliver turned off the lights.

FOUR WEEKS LATER

JANUARY 2006

Fawn—

Enclosed is a photograph of Jill, Matty and myself taken just before Christmas at the beach with the people we love most. I won't tell you anymore, but our smiling faces should answer any questions you have about our happiness.

This is the last time you will ever hear from me.

—Kelly

NINE YEARS LATER***

SEPTEMBER 2014

My Oliver,

This is the only letter I've written since I've been here. I haven't seen or spoken to you since the trial and I'm not sure how to get in touch with you, so I'll send this to your old studio in Denver. Hopefully it will reach you somehow, and hopefully you'll read it.

Six months ago, the prison library <u>finally</u> got a copy of the book Kelly wrote about us. I've read it a lot. The way Kelly described us—and my crimes—was honest and accurate and much kinder than I expected or deserved. She really captured how special and important and beautiful you are . . . and how badly I hurt you.

I'm sorry, Oliver. For everything. That means nothing, I'm sure, as it doesn't change anything or give back anything I took from you, but please know I've never had anything but <u>love</u> for you. You were the greatest love of my lifetime, a lifetime that is about to end.

I've withdrawn my appeals and fired my lawyer. My execution is scheduled for October 12. Like you said, I'm going to die for what I've done, and I'll die almost twenty years to the day since we first met. I've made peace with dying, just not with the solitaire of it.

They've asked me if I have any special requests for my last day. I've asked for Dr. Pepper and movie theatre popcorn—the same snack you and I shared at Dino's Drive-In on our first date in 1994.

I've listed your name—and only yours—on my visitor's list for my execution. When I die, I want to see your face in the witness room. I have no right to ask this of you, but I want your Paul Newmans to be the last things I see in this life. If you aren't there when the curtain opens, I will understand. But I hope you'll consider it.

My ashes will be given to you after my cremation. I would like them scattered behind the Hickory Grove High cafeteria, where you and I first met. I know this too is a huge ask. If you can't do it or simply don't want to, you can refuse and I'll be scattered into the sea instead.

The short time we spent together was the best of my life. I think of it—and you—every day. You've kept me going all these years and I thank you for that, Oliver.

I hope life has treated you well and you've found happiness and love. You deserve nothing but pure joy, because that's what you gave me.

See you soon?

With all the love I have left to give,

Grant

***STAMPED: REFUSED/RETURN TO SENDER**

SUDDENLY ALIVE

ALIVE

SKOT HARRIS

ACKNOWLEDGMENTS

Many thanks and much love to the following people for their support, inspiration and patience as I finished this trilogy: Karl David Woods, Jessica "Nessie" Traynor, Melissa "Missy" Allgood, Joe "Jersey" Skarz, Angelique Mark, Nikki "Louise" Murray, Lorenzo "LoLo" Errico, my LP/Shinoda Family, and my beloved Mom and Pops.

SKOT HARRIS has a degree in creative writing from the University of Michigan. *Suddenly Alive* is his fifth novel. He grew up near Detroit and lives in England with his husband.

EMAIL
skotharris@gmail.com

INSTAGRAM
@skotharris

NEED HELP?
KNOW SOMEONE WHO DOES?

IN THE UNITED STATES

The Campaign to Change Direction
www.changedirection.org

National Suicide Prevention Lifeline
1-800-273-TALK (8255)
www.suicidepreventionlifeline.org

The Trevor Project
1-866-488-7386
www.thetrevorproject.org

IN THE UNITED KINGDOM

Samaritans
116 123
www.samaritans.org

Campaign Against Living Miserably (CALM)
0800 58 58 58
www.thecalmzone.net

MIND—For Better Mental Health
0300 123 3393
www.mind.org.uk

Printed in Poland
by Amazon Fulfillment
Poland Sp. z o.o., Wrocław